Early Praise for Made Ov Me

In Book 3 *Made Ov Me* of his *Journey of a Dark Shaman* trilogy Dale Allen-Rowse once again has expertly given us an unrelenting exploration of a tormented soul, Jack Daw, whose story is continued in this book. As we navigate through the darkest recesses of the human heart and psyche Allen-Rowse carefully defines the barriers between dream and desire, imagination and reality. It's about love and hate and Jack's fascinating self searching spiritual journey. It's told with such vivid imagery one can almost see the narrative unfold on a movie screen, even when it becomes too intense or painful. By the end of this book you will have experienced something that will stay with you for a long time. Dale Allen-Rowse is an electrifying storyteller whose approach is bold, ambitious and always intriguing. I can not wait to see what comes next from this amazing author.

Armand Mastroianni
Producer/Director

As a filmmaker, I'm utterly awestruck by the cinematic qualities of Dale Allen-Rowse's *Journey of a Dark Shaman* trilogy. The third installment, *Made Ov Me,* is nothing short of a revelation. The author's imagination truly knows no bounds. He takes us on the ride of a lifetime, providing an extraordinary roadmap for our own spiritual transformation. It's a visual and auditory feast that never disappoints. After having followed hero Jack Daw's journey to its breathtaking conclusion, my own conceptual horizons have been broadened. I very much look forward to where this author's incredible journey takes us next!

Brad Carpenter – Emmy Nominated TV Producer
Fosse/Verden | Boardwalk Empire | Kaleidoscope | Tokyo Vice

MADE OV ME

JOURNEY OF A DARK SHAMAN TRILOGY

BOOK 3

DALE ALLEN-ROWSE

WOLF VISION PUBLISHING, LLC
MOUNTAIN CENTER, CA

Wolf Vision Publishing, LLC
P.O. Box 157
Mountain Center, California

www.DaleAllenRowse.com

ISBN (book): 979-8-9873971-2-1
ISBN (ebook): 979-8-9873971-3-8

DEDICATION

I would like to dedicate *Made Ov Me* to the dystonia warriors of the world. Our condition is greatly under-funded and under-researched. I hope my story brings some light to this neurological movement disorder—the third most common after Parkinson's and Multiple Sclerosis (MS).

"I have learned so much from God that I can no longer call myself
a Christian, a Hindu, a Muslim, a Buddhist, a Jew. The Truth
has shared so much of Itself with me that I can no longer call
myself a man, a woman, an angel, or even a pure Soul. Love has
befriended me so completely, it has turned to ash and freed me of
every concept and image my mind has ever known."

~ HAFIZ

TABLE OF CONTENTS

WALL

Ding.

Midair, the airplane fasten seatbelt sign switched off as an announcement was made, and a few passengers stood to head for the restrooms.

"We need to talk," Jack said to his newly minted husband.

"Okay," Thad said, settling into his seat. "I have a feeling I know what about, but tell me anyway."

Jack chose his words carefully. "Last night…" He got quiet to get honest. "Last night, during our wedding ceremony, there were some things that, well, I'd like to talk about."

Thad nuzzled his chestnut beard in close so they could talk quieter. "I gotcha, mate." He winked an ever-green eye.

"Well, it's not that exactly," Jack said flatly. "It's…" He reached for a new place to gain clarity and spoke from his higher mind. "The Anam Cara. Is that a spell?"

"A spell?!" Thad said through a giggle in a loud, close whisper.

"I'm serious," Jack said, pushing away.

"Mate…" Thad reached in for closeness but again was rejected.

"Thaddeus Harold Pierson-Daw." Jack folded his arms, indicating he was mostly serious. "You don't get to wiggle out of this one. You need to start answering more of my questions directly!"

"Such as?" Thad lingered, still enjoying their mostly fake fight. Jack took in the proximity of them, and how grounded in Earth-things his husband was. For the rest of his days, Jack would never tired of Thad's grounding energy, red hair and arms so massive they made him feel safe.

"Such as… is the Anam Cara a spell?"

Thad rearranged himself to see Jack better. "Oh, you're serious?"

"Yes, very serious. You know, for someone who says they don't do secrets, you are often full of them." Jack mumbled with a strong side eye toward his love.

Thad adjusted in his chair as an awkward laugh escaped him. "I'm an open book."

"Oh sure, when asked directly. But c'mon…you can't expect me to lead on some of this stuff when it seems you're already halfway down the road. You need to step up and shed some light here. Out with it. All of it—most especially the part about the…" Jack shoulder checked the space for eavesdroppers, "…advanced class. Thad! What the fuck was that? How is what I think I saw, even possible?"

Thad scanned the enclosed space. "Maybe we should wait until we get home to have this conversation. How are you feeling?"

Jack swatted his mate. "Do not redirect. I feel fine." The man occupying the window seat belched loudly, as Jack closed his eyes and finished his thought. "Okay. Maybe this can wait until we get home, but be warned. I am formulating questions the entire ride."

Thad leaned back in his chair and closed his eyes. "Okay, Jack. I got you."

Later that evening at dinner, as was customary, they had themselves arranged out on the back patio overlooking the woods. Jack finally asked, "Can we talk about it now?"

Thad exhaled into the cold near-Christmas night. "Sure." He said while pulling another blanket over them.

"Because it sometimes feels like you have secrets when you're the one who is so against them. It's super confusing to me, Thad. You want this high-minded relationship. Your aim for us has always been 'Zenith's Peak'…to see how far we can take our truth-telling."

"Yes," Thad confirmed. "Ooh. Did you ever finish it?"

"What? Your book?"

"Yes," Thad confirmed. "You mentioned once that your signed copy was stolen before you could finish the last few chapters."

"Fine. I'll grab a copy from your office, but again, you're redirecting. Tell me why you're so cloak and dagger with your intentions and why I get these glimpses of you…that somehow aren't you—or don't represent a version of you that I understand. Level with me. What is the Anam Cara? Why were you so desperate to mark me as your husband and bond us forever? And the sex afterward when it was just us? I need to understand if there is anything to that. You were saying words my mind couldn't process or weren't English."

The outdoor space fell to quiet. "You're right, but you were…you've always said you're okay with us still being physical, even when you're only partially conscious. I mean, it sometimes helps. Right? Brings you around sometimes? Just trust that it's all for the best."

"Thad!" Jack complained. "You don't get to do that. You don't decide what's best for me."

Thad grabbed the attention back. "Remember when we took our first and second trips to the basement of our home?"

Jack laughed. "Ya. Not something I'll soon forget."

"I explained that I don't do secrets, but there are things that I need to know that you're either ready for or…"

"What?!" Jack interjected. "And you think you're the one to make that decision?" A silent second passed. "You're going to decide what I should know unilaterally? That's called a secret, Thad. To me, that accusation is also a confession."

"Hey, mate," Thad assured. "It's not like that."

"Then what is it like?"

Thad exhaled into the stars. "We've talked some about my personal exploration, and you know my early fascination with the evolution of the soul."

"Yes. You understand what I survived and vice versa. Ya…it's why we're so perfectly weird together."

Thad laughed. "Indeed. Well, I found some other things through my explorations."

"Such as?" Jack encouraged.

"Such as, I want you to spend some time with my friend Rosalyn."

"The shaman!" Jack yelled, making them both laugh.

"Yes. She was my master teacher, and rarely have I known anyone with such personal power. I studied with her for almost five years."

"Well… after she understood you weren't trying to blow up her office with a bomb." They both snickered and grinned, remembering the story from Thad's autobiography, Zenith's Peak.

Jack's mind wandered. He lost his gaze into the stars while he remembered back to the powers Dr. Rosalyn Thames demonstrated during their wedding ceremony. Jack concurred, "She is a force."

"That she is, my dearest one. That she is. The two of you can have some time together while I'm on my next trip come this April, but she can't be here for my turnaround to Cache Creek tomorrow."

"Why does this feel like a good news/bad news sort of thing?" Jack asked. "I mean, I know that your big trip is coming together, but your trip tomorrow is just two nights." Jack probed further, sensing there was more. "Were you thinking that someone should be here for me while you're gone, or are you cool with just doing our usual phone thing? Is this time with Rosalyn a dangling carrot? What are your thoughts on that given…the current state of things." They both knew the state of Jack's neurological deterioration. There was no more hiding it.

"Ya, mate. Listen, Jack, I think we need to be honest that someone needs to be with you. Ya, we have the cameras and your medic alert devices and all, but you're just too unstable these days. And it's unfair to ask Nancy, to be here and take on more than she already is with keeping the house running. Maybe things will get better over the next few months as we chase down solutions for you, but I have to be honest, mate. I'm not comfortable with you being alone, not even just for the next two nights. Besides, it's Christmas. I don't want you alone. You should be with family."

Jack got quiet as he felt the imposition of others 'scheduling him'. Thad's intention wasn't free of fear, and it was a fear that Jack wanted to live free of. He wasn't handicapped. Not to his mind. He was simply a person who had a few special care instructions—no need to be more complicated than that. *I can still hang*, he tried to convince himself. *If they'd let it be true... maybe*, Jack told himself.

"Jack?" Thad prompted.

"What did you have in mind?" Jack asked, being as open as he could, despite his latent annoyance.

Thad cozied in closer for a saccharine-flavored nuzzle. "I have it all worked out."

"Thaddeus Harold Pierson-Daw, what is this crazy you're brewing?" Jack squawked into the night.

Thad continued to magic-eyebrow Jack, who laughed despite himself.

"Lunatic!" Jack screamed to the stars. They both laughed and drunk-cuddled under blankets in the cool of the Canadian night air.

"But seriously...Jack, love." He took Jack's face before continuing, "I've asked a few friends to stay with you while I'm away." Jack's cheeks started to sting with anticipation. "But to get all of the days covered," Thad paused and looked deeply into Jack's hazel eyes, "I had to ask your brother to stay the next two nights," Thad said quickly. "And he agreed, so we're good." Thad smiled, attempting to cajole an upbeat response, but Jack's heart sank.

"You fucking did what?!" Jack sat up and turned to face his husband wide-eyed.

"Look, babe, it's Christmas. I hate that I have to do this turnaround, but it's the biggest opportunity of the year. I can't turn down speaking at this big of a gig, not when I've missed so many others …."

"Thad! There is no way in hell I will spend whatever time I have left on earth in that man's presence."

"Wow…it's like that for you, is it?" Thad absently laughed into the space between them. "Really, Jack?" he asked in disbelief. "Not even for me? I don't feel okay with you being alone right now."

Jack turned his back to Thad, crossed his arms, and lowered his head.

Thad reached to stroke his shoulder. "C'mon." Jack wasn't unclenching or opening. "Jack?" Thad tried again, shaking him. "Don't be like this." He tried to turn Jack to face him, but he wouldn't budge. "Talk to me. I'm sorry if that was, you know, over-reaching, but he's family. And I hate that the two of you have abandoned any possibility of a path forward."

The newfound tension in the night made for a terse conversation. It was simply a matter of waiting it out.

"Let's go to bed," Thad finally suggested as Jack stood and began clearing the dishes, stacking the plates, glasses, cutlery, and even tucking the Christmas centerpiece onto one arm. He then rudely winked in Thad's direction.

"Don't worry about it, mate. I can handle it," Jack said as he walked into the kitchen, dropped the stack of dishes onto the counter with one solidly loud put-down, and headed for the bedroom alone.

"Yikes," Thad exclaimed into the night.

SCHEDULE

The morning after, Jack helped Thad shower as the topic of conversation known as "Ben," or Jack's very Christian brother, came up again.

"Jack?" Thad began. "Let's just find a solution. Okay? No—"

"I feel very betrayed," Jack injected loudly, silencing the enclosed tiled space. Thad's face contorted with guilt. "I will not spend time with that man."

Thad reached for Jack, who pulled away into the steam. "He's family, Jack… It's just two nights." Silence. "C'mon, love. Give him a chance."

"Not in this house, if you wish me here." Jack wasn't budging. He was a virtual car crash of emotion as tears teetered below the surface.

"So tell me what can work," Thad offered in a hopeful tone while plumes of shower steam rose. "Name it."

Jack softened a bit to reach for an ounce of wonder. "I hate that you're doing this. I hate that you're forcing this on me. I don't want any part of this, and I need you to have my back. My brother is not a safe place for me, and it is very triggering for me to be in his presence. I will be a huge mess, Thad. Huge!" Jack shifted to face his husband. "You know that kind of angst and social anxiety will physically harm me. That's what you're putting on me. Tonight. With no warning."

He vacated the shower, grabbed a towel, and headed to the closet and down the hall, not saying goodbye.

"Babe, I'm leaving for the airport soon…" Thad called after him, but on the days Jack's legs worked, he could outpace his husband in a single stride.

Twenty minutes later, Thad entered the second bedroom, where Jack sat behind his computer. "Okay, mate, I'm off." A pang of sadness swept them both.

Jack stood and crossed the room. "Ugh. I hate this part."

"I know, mate. I'll be home early Christmas morning, probably before you're even up, and I have the rest of my trips covered. Here's a list of who'll be staying with you for my April and May trips."

"Thad," Jack stopped him but then decided to back off from telling his husband to shove his organized spreadsheet up his fucking ass.

"Ya?" Thad dared.

"Never mind." Jack normally would offer to carry Thad or perform some other Herculean feat of strength to prove he wasn't crippled, but today his sadness over his husband leaving arrested his energy level. "Thanks for taking care of this."

In front of the house, Jack and Nancy, the caregiver and housekeeper, got Thad into the Suburban with the tinted windows, and within a minute, Jack stood at their front door alone. He went back inside to revisit the blank page on his computer.

Sitting down to face the reality found staring back at him, Jack had one thought. Don't think. Just write. Start. Begin. *Whatcha got, you crazy bastard?* he asked himself. He leaned back in his chair, blinking rapidly at the ceiling. "Family," he scoffed. "I'll never understand the point." Jack sat upright. There was a newfound whir in his fingers. He started typing.

So my husband thought, in his infinite wisdom, that I should be assigned a babysitter…

He did this without talking to me. He did this unilaterally, which feels like a massive betrayal of my trust. I'm not okay with this.

Jack's perturbed state hindered his flow, so he stood and decided to take Joy for a walk in the woods behind their new prefab home—it was one of the more notable modern architectural feats of Gambier Island. But first, he grabbed for Thad's babysitting schedule to review it for further cuts or digs.

Dec 23rd & 24th - Ben.

"Fuck!" Jack grabbed to tear the paper in half. He wanted a different reality, but then he quickly read:

April 1-5 – Rosalyn

May 3-5 - Jonathan.

This information stopped him mid-tear. *He wants me to hang out with his ex? Seriously?* He tore the paper into pieces, left the room, and grabbed Joy's leash off the hook by the door. His state of "go fuck yourself" fully animating his every move.

DOORBELL

Ding dong.

Fuck, Jack thought, grabbing for his pants. He had been feeling off and hoped a quick nap might shake him clear, but the afternoon got away from him. Ben and his already regrettable evening were now upon him.

"Hi," Jack said, opening the door to come face-to-face with his much taller, painfully straight sibling for the first time in over a decade. They exchanged a quick and awkward hug as Jack showed Ben into the house.

The two brothers did their best to exchange pleasantries, but each step forward felt like a step back—a step back into old worn and known troughs of privilege. A thing only one brother was attuned with. Like Jack, Ben had been a serious athlete in his younger days. His six foot plus and hefty frame, made him a natural at rugby, whereas Jack with the leaner, smaller build was more adept at track and field. Jack often remembered how their physical difference began the tear of them as brothers and 'family'.

"Nice to be with you on this blessed day," Ben said sincerely. Hearing this, Jack cringed, already irritated by the fact that not one word could be exchanged without bringing God or religion into it.

"Nice to be with you?" Jack asked. *Gah. What does that even mean? Ugh. This guy is so…what?* He considered how to finish that sentence and then landed on *Jonestown.*

"Wow, Jack," Ben said as he continued to make himself at home in the space by flopping on various furniture pieces then rifling through a few closets. "Great place. Is it your friend's?"

Jack took a deep breath. "Yes. This is the home I share with my husband." Jack blinked without moving, letting his words hang in the air with its scented fruit punch.

"Ah, yes. Of course," Ben replied as the awkward buzz of the room found a higher pitch. "Sorry I couldn't…you know."

"Make the wedding?" Jack offered flatly. "All good." Jack didn't bring up that he wasn't invited.

Jack led Ben through a quick tour of the last rooms on the main floor and then decided a beer on the patio might kill some time.

Once they settled outside, beers in hand, his brother said, "So brother…." Jack twisted in his direction in the day's last light. "I appreciate you, you know, getting together. It's been a long time."

The outside garden lighting found its queue and splashed light beams at their designated targets, the yard and open protected green space coming to life in the night.

Jack exhaled. He needed to quell the internal roll of his fired-up ego, so he popped up to his higher consciousness for a breath of clean air. He deliberately breathed and then took in the cooling of the day when he, for the briefest of seconds, saw Ben at his core.

He saw how disturbed his brother was living in a world so steeped in judgment. Jack was just visiting this very dense and dank crazy town. His brother lived there full time—no breaks. Jack, for a second, even saw how, in a way, his brother was a victim of his chosen circumstances. In his brother's world, there was no finding your own holiness and standing in the knowledge of your personal empowerment. Ben would never know what it's like not to serve a lord but to be one with and a part of anima and all that that means.

In Ben's world, dense phases such as, "We're all sinners" or "We're all born sinners" were commonplace. In Ben's world, they lapped at this impenetrable dank pool of dark self-flagellation, self-loathing, and judgment, and he could see how his brother had placed his beliefs in that which flogs and torments daily.

Jack, for a moment, saw that his version of getting beaten translated directly to Ben's. They were the same product of the same pathology that named sons as sinners and daughters as whores.

Jack breathed back the oncoming night where he forced himself to be willing to hear something new and know a new truth. He could do that if he cared to, but the question was twofold. One, did he want to? And two, was there a new foundation to build on, or would his brother seek to rebuild on the same old rank, bigoted ways—the ways that named Jack's marriage as anything less than holy?

Jack tried a smile and replied, "It has been a long time. How is the family?" The words tasted bitter in his mouth as Jack slugged at his beer for chemical confidence while his low-grade neuro-storm sloshed on in the background.

"Heather's good, you know, and the kids....Ya, they're adjusting to life in the States. It's a big switch for them—new schools and all."

"Well, God Bless America." Jack toasted toward nothing in particular.

Ben stared blankly into the distance for a moment. "Ya, well, so what's going on with you and....?"

"Thad?" Jack swallowed more of an unseen insult. *Keep it clean, Jack*, he told himself. *Your character is what you do in this type of situation. Will you let things grow and move beyond the past? Will you allow for something new?* Jack wasn't sure.

"Ya." Ben laughed at the night. "Never known a Thad. What's that kind of a name? Like Australian or something? Anyhow, we've enrolled the kids in a good Catholic school."

Jack remembered his sister-in-law is Catholic, not Baptist, as he and Ben were raised.

"They seem to like it fine." Ben finished his beer and set it on a nearby table.

Well, that's nice, Jack thought, fuming, unsure what else to say about an institution that still names him as "intrinsically immoral and contrary to the natural law," or at least that's what it says on The Archbishop of America's official website.

"So…" Ben tried, before letting a silent beat pass. "Are we good?"

Jack straightened his posture. "What do you mean, good?" he asked, doing his best to keep it clean of ick and ego.

"You know… like no hard feelings and stuff?"

"Well, sure," Jack answered. "You know, the past is no longer a nuisance to be…." He thought hard about whether to name a thing as a thing in the presence of someone blind to his heart's delicate issue.

Jack felt a turning inside him as his feminine heart clarified his mind. *I am whole. I am present. I am divine, and because of that, I know that I must create a path forward with clarity.* His internal voice was calling on the vibration of Meheegan, the white wolf who stood as a lens for Jack to know the divine. Jack summoned her and his courage, thinking, *what would Reason do? What would the advanced class do?*

Jack continued, "Ben, I need to be honest with you. You are not a safe place for my family and me. In the past few minutes, you've already demonstrated how you are a threat to my personal safety more times than I can count. So if you're asking me if we're good for stuff that has happened in the past? Yes. We are good. But that doesn't mean that your behavior in the past, hasn't wounded me in a profound and life-altering way, and that's not nothing… so we're going to call a thing a thing. I know you did your best. I know you're doing your best now.

I know you're learning, too, same as me, but you are not now, nor will you ever be, a safe place for me. Furthermore, while I forgive you for turning on me and abandoning me, I will never forget how quickly you dismissed my humanity and forgot that I was a person. You did that. You vilified me, and there's no possibility that our relationship can recover from that until you undo your core beliefs that I, as a queer person, am less than you or that my marriage is less than yours and Heather's." Jack turned in his chair. "Humans who can deny others the identification of their personhood are a special kind of evil—an evil that has no room here under this roof."

The stunned silence on the patio could be felt for miles.

"So, ARE WE good?!" Jack yelled. "YES. We're as good as we're ever going to be because this, with us chatting about superficial bullshit, is ALL we will ever share. I need us to be clear on that. There is no relationship on the table beyond that until you abandon that which justifies hate against me—which, in this specific instance means your bigoted faith community. You know, the one that labels queer expression as "an abomination" in the eyes of God AND literally calls for followers of the bible to kill any two men that they find having sex."

Jack could feel the presence of the white wolf leaning into her vicious snarl that lived just beneath his surface. The air murmured with her murderous silence.

Ben looked dumbfounded, like he had been slapped stupid. He eventually replied, "Where have you learned to be so outright bigoted and hateful?"

"Jesus, here we go…" Jack rolled his eyes.

"Jack!" Ben exclaimed. "You will not take our father's name in vain. You need to apologize!"

"For what? For saying that you're putting your children into a horrifically bigoted institution of the Catholic Church to indoctrinate them against my family? Or because you adopted a faith that I know the ins and outs of? You don't get to say otherwise. You don't get to say that you and your religion stand for goodness and helping others because I know it's not! I was there when we learned this judgey horseshit, Ben. I was there when our minds were poisoned with the concept of terror found through sin. I was there."

The space between the two men ionized anew as a different tone struck a chord that tethered back generations. Ben stood and leapt at Jack, who dropped his beer. They both fell and slammed into the cold concrete pavers, lighting a new path for Jack's already rapidly declining mental abilities.

Twinge.

God damn it! Jack thought, as he tried to regain his footing. He was not at all surprised by this violent turn of events from his brother, whose life was guided by a personally prescribed sense of moral righteousness to his core.

The race was underway, Ben to convince Jack to right his wrong and Jack to deal with anything physical before it all melted away. Such was the way in the Daw family, and no one expected anything different. On his knees, Ben quickly grabbed Jack by the neck as they again, tumbled to the ground.

Jack panicked and hit his medic alert device, sending a message to others offsite. He knew what came next, and hated that this was his reality.

SEIZED

Ben's weight crushed Jack's mid-section on the cold concrete patio. "Apologize!" Ben yelled.

"For what?!" Jack managed through the jumble of limbs and clothes. "Speaking the truth?"

"Jack, you're not making any sense. Why would you say that!?"

"Say what? That you're enrolling your kids into an institution of bigotry and hate? Because you fucking are! And you need to understand that when you belong to AND FUND institutionalized bigotry against my family, I view it as a direct threat." The words they exchanged tumbled and rolled as they did.

Ben's larger footballers-frame quickly pinned Jack on his back while Jack rallied to get his words out while he still had breath.

"If your church held the same beliefs toward black people as they do toward my family and me, would you stay?" Silence. "WELL, bigot?!"

"What?!" Ben screamed in confusion. They paused to catch their breath as Jack covered his head, fending off any potential blows. "What bigotry? What are you even talking about?"

Jack relaxed mid-struggle, removing his arms from his head in protection mode. "Does your fucking Jesus book say that men who fuck men—queers, homosexuals, sodomites, and non-binary people—are an abomination? Are Jews an abomination? How about black people? Are they an abomination? If what is said about ME in your circles was said about Jews or black people, would you still attend? TELL ME! Where's the line for your hate? It's on their fucking website," Jack screamed, recalling the memorized text. "The Catechism of the Catholic Church, a text that contains dogmas and teachings of the Church, names homosexual acts as intrinsically immoral and contrary to the natural law, and names homosexual tendencies as objectively disordered."

Hearing this, Ben again heaved at Jack, whose struggle was egging on a neurological episode.

"But I bet you can't hear that. I bet you think those words are okay to describe my family and me. But let me be clear." They stopped wrestling as Jack let loose. "The Catholic faith is a God-damned hate group based on white supremacy. Between hiding rapists and vile child predators to their outright horrific bigotry, they are not in ANY way godly. Let me phrase what they have on their website another way, Ben. The Catechism of the Catholic Church names black people as intrinsically immoral and contrary to the natural law and names people of color as objectively disordered. But it's just us faggots, so who cares, right? RIGHT?!"

Ben stood and offered a hand in Jack's direction, who stood and dusted himself off. "Where's all of this coming from, Jack? Why are you so full of hate?"

The dystonic nature of the two worlds collided, where neither party could make sense of the other's perspective. The moment reverberated with queerness, each party hearing nothing but pure hate in their brother's words. Jack searched for one commonly held shred of reality.

"You don't get to request that I abide by your institutionalized hate! Love is defined as the absence of judgment," Jack said as Ben made his way back to his barstool, his anger visible as he finally tried to listen.

"God is love," Ben clarified.

"NO! Fuck your God! Your God is small, punitive, and judgmental. Your God has NOTHING to do with love, at least not that I've seen. Your God isn't love. Love is love," Jack fired back.

The moment rang silent for half a second, giving the men's minds time to regain a modicum of shared common sense.

"Jack, you're not making sense. When did you become such a fucking bigot? I expected more from you than being anti-Christian. You weren't raised to be this hateful."

And there it was. The split. The fracture and the schism of realities. Jack had been raised to be this hateful, as was Ben. The ferocity of their expressions verified this truth while they savagely reviewed their next move in this well-known dance of ugly, ego-driven righteousness.

Ben clarified, "I am a good Christian, Jack." Then he scoffed, "More than I can say for you."

"You are Ben. You are an EXCELLENT Christian—a model Christian… and a fucking horrible person. That is YOUR truth. That is my experience of you."

Ben stammered a response. "What?!" Then he yelled, "That doesn't even make sense, Jack. I know you have all these fucking mental problems… I'm sorry, but that doesn't give you the right to be this evil. What is wrong with you?"

Jack stood to tower over Ben, who sat at the outdoor bar, cornering the taller brother in place.

"WHAT IS WRONG WITH ME?! What is wrong with me?" Jack could feel his internal dystonic writhing movements begin as a red light started to blink on the home camera that faced the patio. He started to tremble, which encouraged the destruction of his remaining senses. An electric twinge then ran down Jack's right side, short-circuiting connections under its slither.

Ben's face visibly registered the sight of the wriggling movement, which stopped and plainly alarmed him.

Jack continued, "What's wrong with me is that I was born into your world a sin. I was born into your world as a crime. You saw that I was different, and you attacked it. You festered with the truth of me being born onto the queer spectrum, and you and your fellow Christians let that judgment rot in your minds until you had to kill it." Jack chose his next words carefully. "I have never seen an ounce of compassion or kindness from you, Mom, or Dad. Not one. That won't be forgotten. You will never be a safe place for me."

Ben muttered into the night, "'Proverbs 22:15. Foolishness is bound in the heart of a child, but the rod of correction shall drive it far from him.' That's our charge, Jack. Why is that bad…to be of service to the Lord?"

"Of service?!" Jack exclaimed, the notion deeply stuck in a mire of repellant ass-hattery. "To whom? To Christian nationalism?! Your ego? By the fucking way…the verse right before that is, 'The mouth of the adulterous woman is a deep pit; a man who is under the Lord's wrath falls into it.' This feels right to you? To lead your life from a book that says such dense misogynistic statements? Or how about the rank misogyny of 1 Corinthians 14:34, 35—As in all the congregations of the saints, women should remain silent in the churches. They are not allowed to speak, but must be in submission, as the Law says. If they want to inquire about something, they should ask their own husbands at home; for it is disgraceful for a woman to speak in the church!" The two brothers sat in silence for a moment before Jack continued. "How about 'And Hazel said, 'Why does my lord weep?' He answered, 'Because I know the evil you will do to the people of Israel. You will set on fire their fortresses, and you will kill their young men with the sword and dash in pieces their little ones and rip open their pregnant women.' THIS FEELS RIGHT TO YOU?!!"

"JACK!" Ben looked like he was doing his best to remain seated. "That is God's word!"

"Ya… and a word I know inside and out." Jack knew he could out-Bible his block of a brother who never had a head for actual knowledge or facts. The man was a very large parrot at best. "God's word, eh?" Jack rolled into his saved Rolodex of "go fuck your god." "Deuteronomy 25: 11-1," he continued. "'If two men are fighting and the wife of one of them comes to rescue her husband from his assailant, and she reaches out and seizes him by his private parts, you shall cut off her hand. Show her no pity!'" Jack wasn't letting up.

"JACK!" Ben yelled again, to be met with the next verse in Jack's database of verses.

"HUMAN TRAFFICKING. Exodus 21. When a man sells his daughter as a slave, she will not be freed at the end of six years as the men are. If she does not satisfy her owner, he must allow her to be bought back again."

Ben's face betrayed his anger as Jack's scream of offense. "NUMBERS 31. 'Now, therefore, KILL every man among the little ones AND KILL EVERY WOMAN WHO HAS KNOWN MAN INTIMATELY. BUT ALL THE GIRLS WHO HAVE NOT KNOWN MAN INTIMATELY, SPARE FOR YOURSELVES.'" Jack lost himself down the rabbit hole of past pains and gutted angst. "Again, I ask…. This feels right to you?"

Ben slapped back with, "Well, you can't just point out the bad parts of the Bible!"

"Bad parts?! You, who just said this ancient text is the 'Word of God,' now says that GOD wrote his text with 'bad parts.' Am I getting that right? Did he need a better editor!?" Jack laughed.

Ben slowed to review the question as Jack asked, "So who magically decides what parts of the Bible are good and which are bad? Or better yet, which parts are ACTUAL fucking history in the same manner as you're teaching your children, such as your little glory trip to see Noah's Ark built to scale with cages and cages of dinosaurs?" Jack was wide-eyed in his pissed-off state. "Cause here's the fucking problem! You have no access to self-assessment or critical thought. You have NO access to actual right and wrong regarding what love is. You look at my marriage and don't see love. You see sex. Why? I don't consider what you and Heather share as a sexual offering. Why do you do that to me?"

"Your marriage is an affront to the Church."

And there it was. The words hung in the cool air. Both men stayed silent as their stench filled the space between them.

"Yes. It. Is," Jack choked with an unmoving steel in his voice. "Leviticus 20:13. 'If a man lies with a male as with a woman, they have committed an abomination; the two of them shall be put to death; their bloodguilt is upon them.' 'Cause you know what? There isn't a queer man alive who hasn't heard this yelled at them while getting their face kicked in. 'Says so in the Bible!' they jeer, because that verse is all the justification bullies need to beat us until we're dead. In their minds, they're literally doing 'God's work'—but you probably have absolved yourself. You probably have determined that your actions have nothing to do with gay men getting killed in the streets, despite belonging to it AND funding it."

Jack could feel tears trail down his cheeks as the overwhelm of unfairness grew. This was the final straw, and the white-hot pain of his brother's myopic vision depleted his last shred of resistance. Jack's face untethered from its normal place of hope to ring the bell of palsy. A new resonance of defeat vibrated throughout him. "You can't see love where it exists… and yet you can see the replica of an ancient ship that's 510 feet long and somehow KNOW, with all that you are, that God put two of 8.7 million species of animals on it. If you can look at that, and it makes sense to you, then you have abandoned critical thought. Furthermore, to teach your children that's actual history, that the earth is six thousand years old… is pathetic. You haven't even chosen or decided on your belief system, and you don't question what's right or good. In your world, you 'eat of your savior's flesh and drink of his blood,' and it's <u>not</u> mock cannibalism." Jack could feel that he needed to lie down. His neck scrunched into his right shoulder. "I need to go to bed."

Jack deflated. He had no more fight.

He headed back toward the house and turned for a final comment. "You know, if you had spent as much time searching for your truth in all faiths as you did picking out your last car, I could respect what you do. But you don't. You don't investigate religions and then select that which most closely resonates with you and your values, but rather you just follow in lockstep this fucked-up version of pathology that we were taught. So, it's not exactly the way, the truth, and the light, but rather literally the only fucking thing you know. I meant what I said, Ben. You're an amazing Christian, which, from where I stand, translates directly to you being a fucking lousy human."

As Jack turned to head inside, his legs gave out, and his ribcage contracted hard. Wheezing, Jack glanced back at Ben who exclaimed, "THIS is what Dad spoke of! Father, save us!" Ben blew past his brother's cratering state and returned with his overnight bag, a Bible and police-grade zip ties. "Tonight, this ends. Tonight, I free you, Jack. Hold on, buddy. Dad told me what to do."

BATHTUB

When Ben retrieved his overnight bag from the foyer, Jack grabbed his phone and texted Thad. His fingers were heading offline, but he still managed a three-character message with his knuckle: 9-1-1.

After hitting send, his legs fully gave way and rendered him fully to the cold concrete floor. Jack's functions quickly evaporated, and by the time Ben returned to the outside patio, Jack's ribs continued to contract, turning each rapid exhale into a demented hiss.

Standing before Jack at the door, Ben said quietly, "We don't have much time." Jack watched as Ben pulled item after item from his bag. He had come prepared. Ben was armed to the teeth for this premeditated act. With zip-ties in his big meaty hands Jack's brother paced a circle around him and then abruptly stood frozen with fear. Jack saw his reflection in Ben's eyes as he begged for breath and spat wildly, gasping for air while his rib cage struck an even tighter boa-constricted death blow.

Ben jumped out of the way of Jack's spit. "Your AIDS has no power here. Father!" Ben yelled, sidestepping more of Jack's flying spit while the junior brother's breathing became more audibly rattled.

Jack tried to breathe, but his chest crushed him like a vice. He tried not to fight it. He tried to stay calm and breathe as normally as he could, but his legs were pinned under him in an extremely painful contortion. His body heaped another bucket of cold adrenaline into his veins as his nervous system revolted from the stress and havoc.

Side-stepping Jack's spittle, Ben's eyes flashed wide. He then turned and forcibly struck Jack upside the head, which dislodged his fake eye. Jack watched the large white lens fall beside him.

Ben shouted into the air, "Mark 16:17! THESE signs will accompany those who have believed." The tall blonde man shook his Bible heavenward. "In MY name, they will cast out demons!" He stalked the saber-rattling beast of Jack, who lay hissing on the floor. "I will repair our family name. I will baptize Jack and return him to be a real man of God." He held a police baton in Jack's direction. "Isn't that what you want, Jack? To be made whole again?"

Jack felt the air in the room, heavy with anticipation knowing that Ben was about to do something he'd never been able to do before—make their stepfather proud.

Jack remained conscious and focused on slow, deliberate breathing exercises. He could not fend off Ben's siege. He couldn't communicate or move. He could only accept and experience. That's all Jack had left. Those were his options.

From a bizarre angle, Ben lunged at Jack's throat, as one would approach a wounded crocodile rather than a person in need of medical assistance. Ben stuffed a rag in Jack's mouth, flipped him over, and zip-tied his hands behind his back.

Jack lay silent, and then, he heard Thad's voice screaming through the smart home sound system.

"BEN! NO! He needs help! He's having an attack! BEN!!! BEN!"

Cinching the final tie, Ben claimed, "Now you can't infect me." He dragged Jack into the house. His mind already too intimate with the scars in the flooring—too many attacks already lived down at this level. They cleared the threshold as Jack felt his clothes tug at the grate of the bamboo-wood floor. Passing the kitchen Jack took another gasp at air, but by now his shirt was choking him. He tried to yell but couldn't find air. The recessed lights overhead passing one, then another, down the hall he slid. They entered the bathroom where Ben plopped Jack next to the tub. "I will end this family's bedevilment for good."

MINUTE ONE

As Jack hung onto the last tendrils of consciousness, Ben began filling the tub. His diminishing senses filled with faint receding glimmers of light and the sounds of running water. His vacated eye socket, pink and brownish, scanned for what might come next, but Jack received nothing from it—his operational eye barely receiving more. It was a blur. Then finally, nature's mercy began to surrender him to the warm white void of nothingness. Jack could feel his mind begin to slip.

Ben acted quickly. "C'mon!" he yelled at the tub. His eyes darted back and forth from the water level to Jack on the floor.

Baptists have to fully submerge their disciples, and Ben took to the tub to address the water and its sanctified charge. He pulled a thermos from his bag and emptied it into the warm rising water. *Holy water?* Jack questioned. Ben turned for the dog-eared pages in his Bible.

As Jack slipped into a semi-conscious state, he lost his bowels. *None of this is real,* he thought as he slipped further toward the void, desperately clutching to consciousness, his vision, like seeing through dark frosted glass. Ben turned his face upward as the foul smell filled the space.

His brother used his baritone voice to summon the power of his Lord. "Now what?" Ben asked no one, frustration layered into his voice.

"Hello?" Jack vaguely heard the tinny version of his mother's voice echo in the distance.

"Mom!" Ben yelled excitedly. Jack was sliding toward the dark. "I got him, but my God. You…" Ben paused, seeking the right words. "Dad was right. It's bad. It's got him, but it's showing itself to me now. I think I can, like Dad said, cast it out."

"Reverend!" his mother shouted from the cell phone speaker.

"Son?" It was their stepfather. "Listen to me closely…"

MINUTE TWO

Bang! Bang! Bang! Bang!

Someone pounded on the front door.

"Shit!" Ben leaped off the floor. The banging on the front door continued aggressively, which could only mean one thing. Thad was watching and had called the authorities.

Ben ran through the house, searching to right the unsecured wrongs. He bolted while Joy, the bulldog, barked wildly at the frenzy of commotion.

"I just need more time," Ben mumbled passing the bathroom. He grabbed a bucket in the laundry room.

Heading back into the bathroom, Ben almost tripped over but then snatched at Jack's cane, as he was Able, saying, "No more weakness, Jack." He filled bucket after bucket in the sink to add to the tub's rising level, reciting, "LUKE 11, 20. But if I cast out demons by the finger of God, then the kingdom of God has come upon you." He sang and then cried the words. He asked the heavens, "Bless me to complete thy will. Bless me to have the strength and to have courage." He looked down at Jack who could barely make out the figure towering over him. Jack knew his words were gone. He knew what a severe contraction of the voice box felt like. "I will save you, brother, so we can be as we were." The unsaid part of that statement being, before rights and wrongs were sins, and before love found a fracture—a split that cratered the family into two distinct party lines.

Jack faintly heard Ben crying, offering himself to his God. Then Ben quietly stood and turned off the water.

It was time.

MINUTE THREE

Ben picked up then plunged Jack into the tub. Within half a second, the fire alarm began screeched throughout the home, competing with Ben's jubilant praises. He held Jack's head above water as the murk of his feces ran rampant with liquid gravity. Ben's eyelids peeled back in terror as he realized that Jack was conscious again, and he was wide eyed with terror.

Ben yanked the sock out of Jack's mouth, who gasped, sputtered, and coughed for air. Ben pulled Jack out of the tub and set him on the cool, concrete tiles. Brown water splashed all four bathroom walls. The elder brother grabbed at the phone, which was still on speaker.

"AAAaaa," Jack moaned, coughed, and gasped with his hands bound behind his back. The deafening alarm bells continued their assault, screeching mercilessly making Jack even more terrified in his muddled brain state, where any stimuli is terrifying and painful. He wasn't able to fully process what was happening. Loud stimuli are impossible to process for someone during an attack, it just feels terrifying—there's no other way to put it. Jack's body heaved and then threw up a liter of water onto his chest. He struggled to breathe in the shit-stinking pandemonium.

"Father!" Ben yelled through the chaos of the blaring emergency horns. The approved son tried again. "Father!" The cry came from a man unhinged, but then again, he emulated the hum and vibe of the father and Reverend and, in doing so, had adopted both his vibration and his pain. In Ben, it was to live on eternally.

Jack finally found air, and his breathing returned to normal. Gaining some strength and lung capacity, he screamed and wailed for the assault to stop.

However, his hands were still cuffed behind him. There was little he could do—his slowed brain again, then finally fixed at a preverbal state. The unintelligible gibberish spewed on through spittle and vomit as brokenness. Ben's expression verified that the demon was back.

Just as before, just like his father, Ben tried to save Jack and failed. Jack wasn't fixed or whole yet, and there was no more room for error.

Ben reached for his gun.

MINUTE FOUR

Jack tried recovering his breath as he realized he didn't have access to language. He gained a sliver of vision. Ben waved around crosses, holy water… and a gun.

"Arguu beeto…!" Jack screamed, desperate to be understood.

"You speak in tongues!" Ben took Jack by the shoulders and, in a single move, threw him back into the brown murky water.

Jack thought he heard his father rejoice in the background as gallons of tainted brown water were displaced onto the floor. The small enclosure was awash in putrid holy water foulness.

Like being raped, the betrayal cut so deep that Jack disassociated and ceased all caring. He mentally cut his ties to it all, and in that moment, that even meant his ties to Thad. They were all in on it. They had all carried a blind spot to the special care instructions that were woven into Jack's design.

With this thought alone, he slumped, submerged into his brother's brotherly love. *None of this is real,* was his final thought as he accepted lungsful of shit water.

Red and blue shapes and colors suddenly painted the walls. Police sirens whined, ensuring the entire neighborhood was awake and alert to the situation. A bullhorn blared in the yard.

"It's now or never," Ben said, and as a man of God, he would ALWAYS do the right thing. Ben shouted to his maker, "I OFFER

YOU, YOUR CHILD. YOUR CATECHUMEN!" The creature in the dank water splashed and wailed. "We offer you…," Ben turned, "We offer you, Jack."

Ben's incantation continued as Jack felt the water overtake him again.

Help! Jack's mind screamed, but he was on autopilot, the human body's soundtrack of the drowning and dying—sounds we make that we don't recognize. Jack figured if it was his time to go, so be it.

The alarms suddenly ceased as the lights in the home restored to normal, and the strobes disappeared. Ben stopped cold in his tracks.

Jack's mind slipped again. He fully devolved into the mind of an unsafe child, and he cried softly through desperate gasps as his head came out of the water once again.

He finally landed on a word. "Mom," Jack sobbed. She, his mother, was his last hope; the woman who claimed that he had killed his dad because "of how he was." She, the one who said all that, was his last hope. For Jack, there was no expectation of life beyond that.

The otherwise silent room echoed with Jack's quiet pleas.

The police stormed into the room with amazing speed and force and, within one second, had both brothers on the floor but for entirely different reasons. Two brothers—a foot apart, a world of difference—both products of the same rules applied to differing minds in the same vicious and unrelenting manner.

CURTAINS

The following day passed in a blur of misplaced care, legal conversations, and concerned calls. Nancy stayed to help Jack overnight, but by morning, he was back to his regular self.

Thad made a call just before dawn to check in. His voice was strained. "Babe?"

Jack glanced in Nancy's direction. "Thad. We need to talk." The tension in the room grew as Nancy excused herself from their primary bedroom.

Once they were alone, Jack sat on the edge of the bed. "I'm fine… but I'm also really not feeling safe right now."

Thad jumped in. "I know. I'm on my way."

"Thad, I mean us." A new, weighted silence fell between the men. "I'm not feeling safe, and I need some time…and space."

"I'm sorry," Thad replied quietly as he started to cry. The rollercoaster of the past night clearly taking its toll on each man—one now emotional, one now numb. Jack was stone silent and let his husband cry.

When Thad collected himself, Jack clarified, "I think you should stay where you are and finish your trip."

"Jack! No, please."

"Thad." Jack injected a complete sentence. "I need a minute." The room's mood stung with Jack's truth.

"Okay," Thad finally acquiesced.

Jack helped Thad calm down a little. They even managed a sad little laugh over it, but then they were ready to move to their respective corners for a moment to catch their breath.

"Do you want to just...?" Thad questioned, finding no end to the sentence.

"I'll call you tonight." Jack put a hand on his head. "I'm fine, really. I just need a minute. That's all I ask."

"I love you, mate," Thad said after a quick kiss goodbye.

Several hours later, Jack sat in his office speaking with Thad's attorney and longtime friend, Stewart Barrows.

"I don't want to press charges," Jack said boldly. "I'd like to speak with him, but please return him here to the house to get his things. Actually, no. Please have someone come and get his things. I don't want Ben here. Just put him on the phone, and let's be done with it."

"All right," Stewart agreed as they hung up.

Jack's phone rang after only a few minutes. He closed his eyes and felt the hum of himself, the resonance of who he was to the world. He silently asked that if anything good was to come from this situation, it had to be an ending—a complete termination of this nightmare set on repeat that was his family. That could be Jack's only port of safety. He would not offer himself up to any variation where this hellish familial ordeal became his reality. Jack knew he had to love himself enough to allow that this was true for him and his life.

He took a breath and answered the phone. "Hello?" Midday sunshine found a few surfaces around him to alight. The modern architecture of the home bragging of clean lines, sunlight and white.

"Hey," Ben's voice rang into Jack's ear with evident strain.

"Hi."

"Look," Ben tried but then redirected, "Jack, you...."

That was the second Jack flashed to the wolf's white electric anger. That was all it took, just two little words, "Jack" and "you." Jack finally had enough, and it was his turn to be heard.

"Ben!" An awkward moment fell between them. "I am only going to say this once, and I would appreciate it if you would listen AND hear me."

A silent beat buzzed between them.

"I need to separate myself from your world. So let me ask you this." Jack stopped talking to choose the very best words he could devise. "Are you doing the best that you can? Are you really trying to do the right thing?"

Ben stumbled into a "Yes."

"I know you are, Ben, and guess what? So am I. The problem is we live in two completely separate universes. Your reality is not mine, and vice versa. I don't understand how you view what I share with Thad as anything less than holy. HOW DARE YOU, BEN! You come for my family, and I will fucking kill you. Do you HEAR ME?!" Jack fumed, shaking from head to toe.

He stood and found his deepest power and ultimate truth, which came from his feminine heart. Jack leveled up and named it.

"I don't hate you, Ben. I feel sorry for you, BUT I also get you. I get the self-flagellation. I get it. I see it.…. Hell, I know it. And I'm sorry." The air between them was tight with gospel truths. "You are me, only with a different personality and a different set of circumstances. So it calls out one other major difference that I cannot overlook. You turned on me, Ben. You vilified and mocked my feelings, family, and love. I would never do that to you, and while yes, I forgive you for being where you were when you made those old choices, I cannot forget how quickly you invalidated my life. Moving forward, I choose not to see you, not out of spite, but because we have to start somewhere to find any common ground. We have to start with the facts. There is no common ground between us, and trying to create it is causing us harm because, all too often, verbal or otherwise, violence is an option for you. Why? Why is that okay in your mind? I'd never put my hands on you like that. I just don't get it, Ben."

Jack was exasperated as he spoke into the ceiling.

"What do you see in your world? How is it okay to take a device of torture, hang it on the wall, and pray to it? How is it you don't see that as gory and deeply dark and disturbing? How is it that you can pray out of literature that is a fucking horror show against humanity and feel that you're doing the right thing? Have you even read the Bible? Because I fucking have, and it is a fucking atrocity!"

Ben didn't speak. The silence stretched painfully.

"You may purchase male or female slaves from among the foreigners who live among you. You may also purchase the children of such resident foreigners, including those born in your land. You may treat them as property, passing them on to your children as a permanent inheritance. You may treat your slaves like this, but the people of Israel, your relatives, must never be treated this way. Leviticus 25:44"

Jack was losing the struggle to remain decent while years' worth of torment released from deep within himself.

"What do you hear when I say those words, Ben? Does this feel right to you? Do clear instructions on how to hold and trade enslaved people feel appropriate for today's conversations on spirituality? But there it is. You think it's okay to get life advice from literature that names several times when it's appropriate to kill your child. You belong to a horrific institution that normalizes bigotry against queer people, and then you want to tell me you're on my side? Fuck off, Ben! If this is the best you have to offer and bring to the conversation, then no. No, I don't have to respect that choice. I don't have to respect that you choose to belong to a Jesus group with horrendously bigoted views against me. That's not okay for you or your fucking Catholic wife! You both reek of the institution's rampant bigotry. What the hell is wrong with you people?!" Jack cried, vigilant to be heard.

"You don't get a pass. Good people don't belong to bigoted organizations, Ben. How is that not clear to you? Good people DO NOT sit and enjoy the privileged shade of the bigotry tree! How is ANY of this okay? So no… I don't have to bow and scrape to your Jesus. Your faith is cruel and loveless, and I will never respect people who choose to be a part of that vile horseshit."

He paused, very aware of the rise and fall of his labored breathing. He couldn't hold this in any longer.

"It's never okay to lose sight of another's humanity. I need you to know how I feel. Understand that we have no common ground. So let's just let it rest there and find peace. Maybe even trust that the 'other side' is doing the best they can and making the best decisions they can. We're all just trying to do the same, and if we had a checklist from that perspective, suddenly, we'd have unity. Unity is the core common good that benefits all… and I get that to those accustomed to straight white privilege, equality feels like oppression, but you have to trust me a little too. I am not a bad person, Ben. Minorities and immigrants aren't bad people. We're just trying to create our families in a manner that reflects how the creator made us. Where's your trust in that part of God's plan? The part that includes me, my love, and my family?"

Ben exhaled, "Ya."

Jack continued, "So let's dial it all the way down. Participating in a rage campaign benefits neither one of us as hard-working assholes trying to do right for their families. Can we stop and hold a space for the future but know we can't be in each other's lives for a while? Possibly ever."

He slowly rubbed the tense muscles in his neck.

"This crazy making has to end. But I also believe you will never stop vilifying people who are different from you because your privilege requires it. If you can do all this bigoted shit to your own flesh and blood, I can only imagine what you're capable of with strangers. Please realize how xenophobic, homophobic, and racist that makes the world.

People like me just want to feel safe. That's it. I want to hold hands with my husband in all 50 states and every province and territory in North America. But that's not a vision of the world you can share with me because, again, your hate book names me as 'an abomination.'"

"Jack—" Ben started.

"Ben, good-bye. I wish you well. Do not ever call me." Jack then said his final farewell.

Outside, Jack heard someone drive off in Ben's car. He stepped onto the front porch to make sure whoever it was also took his bag. They did.

Jack felt sadly free.

CHIPPED

Jack returned to his office. It, like the rest of the home, was bright, white and wood. He sat at his desk and took in the view overlooking the yard, noting how quiet the house suddenly felt. He settled after an exhale and opened his computer to write. But once again, nothing came to him.

His gaze eventually landed on his reflection in the window. Jack stared at it, at the reflection of him, the one with the missing fake eye and vacant socket. He hated the way that made him feel. It was like the worst part of his attacks. In those moments, he felt like a monster because he scared people—only, unlike an attack, it doesn't fade or change, get better with time, or ever go away. It just hangs there—a gross dead socket. However, these days, he wouldn't let himself think he was "defective," which was notable progress for his mindset.

I don't even know where to begin, Jack thought while the blank screen mocked him. *So I guess I begin by stating that I don't know where to begin.*

On his computer, he typed:

With Ben now gone, I don't know how I feel about things. Nothing feels secure. Well... not Thad because even when I'm mad at him, I can't imagine my life without him. It's more....

Jack had a new thought. *It's more that, I guess, life is just as it is. The world is just as it is… and when the core root of my issue is that people can't or won't hear me, who's to say I can't change that?*

The puzzle in Jack's mind made him ponder a new question. *What if I level up? What if I become a force, one who cannot be misheard or ignored? Now, that might start to change the world.*

He went back to the writing.

But what the fuck does that even mean…? Like, how?
Qualities of someone who can change the world:
1. Bold – someone you can't ignore
2. Has a message…but of what?
3. Clarity
4. Someone…?

Jack chewed the end of his fingernail for a second, losing himself out into the view of the woods. The trees grounding him in his mental wander.

What's my message? he thought. *My wish, like Thad said? No. It's not enough. That's not a story or a message of interest.*

The ping of the word "interest" caught Jack's senses. *Interest… as in interesting.* Jack sat up, reworking back to a half notion swirling in his mind. He rewound the past to arrive back at it. *Interesting. I'm….*

He almost missed it.

"I'm interesting," Jack said aloud. "I mean… I'm not a lot of things… but I am interesting, I guess. I've lived a weird life." Jack noted the past tense of the sentence but let it go. No need to gnaw on that gnat. No need to visit that pool of poison. Not now—possibly ever.

He heard a car pull into the driveway and ran to the window. *Thad's home.*

BIG MAD

The driver helped Thad into the house with the bags while the usual Pacific Northwest expression fell lightly from the sky.

As Jack closed their front door behind his husband, he turned to address the issue. "I asked you not to be here. I said I needed a minute…," Jack exhaled, "after you failed to hear me that my family is not a safe place for me."

Thad approached Jack. "Yes. Forgive me."

The men stared at one another for just a moment before falling into each other's arms. They cried, silently reliving the whole ordeal. Thad repeatedly apologized as they made their way to the kitchen.

"Nancy is here if you…Have you eaten?" Jack asked.

"No, I'm starving. And mostly just happy to be here with you."

"Me, too. I'll grab wine. Nancy cooked a fabulous Christmas Eve feast. Meet you out back?"

"Music to my ears."

Forty-five minutes later, they snuggled under their usual outdoor blankets while the fire pit roared and Nancy plated dinner.

"All set then?" Nancy smiled behind her large round glasses and curly hair. Her usual mom-energy sparking a tad shinier, given the day.

"Thank you," Thad said. "Merry Christmas. Do you have family waiting? Do you need to go?"

Jack quickly added, "Yes, Nancy, we're fine. This is truly amazing."

"Well…I was hoping to catch up with my niece, but I'm not sure she'll make it today." She sighed. "Maybe tomorrow."

"Nancy, we're fine. Go. See you in a few days. We'll text if we run into trouble." Thad winked.

The men's caregiver soon left, and the outdoor patio returned to nature's quiet again. Thad embraced Jack with all his muscled might. "I thought…" Thad started to cry. "I'm so sorry. I'm just so glad you're okay."

"But am I?" Jack asked flatly, unattached to emotion.

"What?" Thad straightened himself and wiped away a stray tear.

"I don't know if I'm okay after that, Thad. What I just went through…because it's always the same. People get to do whatever the fuck they want to me. Then everyone just shrugs it off with a 'Glad you're okay.'"

Jack disconnected and lost his one-eyed vision out into the night.

"You have to level with me, Thad. I need all of it—all the stuff you casually allude to but then never tell me. I want the whole truth. This crazy ritual evolution stuff? What the fuck is that?"

"Okay," Thad said. "Maybe you're right. Maybe it's time to do more than test the theory of Zenith's Peak. Maybe it's time to live it." The older man got serious. His thick-muscled back and arms pulling at his love for connection. "But, Jack, you have to trust that what I'm about to show you is from original source energy."

Jack ran scenarios in his head but, coming up with nothing, asked, "And that's what now?"

"Exactly," Thad confirmed.

"Exactly what?"

"Exactly what I have to show you between now and when Rosalyn arrives." He raised a reddish eyebrow, as his green eyes found a curious animation. "Ready for another trip to the basement?"

"Fuck yes!" Jack screamed, and they both laughed.

OMNISM FOUND

The men made their way into the elevator, the spin of them reckless and drunk. They had long ago given themselves permission to live without rules and restrictions. Sure, it might make for a few extra "problems" along the way—problems that, if they went full granola and lemongrass lifestyle, might lessen. But with Thad surviving and thriving despite his twenty-plus years being HIV+, they simply wanted to live each day, full out, no rules. Whatever felt right, they chose each moment freely.

Thad leaned into Jack for a kiss, pinning him against the elevator wall as the big steel box descended. It bumped to a halt, and the doors slid open. Jack ran to the center of the space and turned back to yell at Thad, who was mid-hobble.

"Right?" Jack looked at the black chests full of witchy wonder. "…Or left?" He smiled and bounced with sexy-trouble energy, indicating to the double doors that walled off the adult dungeon playroom.

Thad replied, "How about both?"

"Ah…okay." Jack quizzically raised an eyebrow. He laughed and said, "Fuck me up."

Thad chuckled. "On all levels—you're game for that?"

Jack met his spouse toe to toe. "Let's get weird."

They both raced in their own ways—Jack to the playroom, grabbing at cables and cuffs, and Thad to the black chests of wonder, picking through items Jack hadn't yet seen or experienced.

"In here!" Jack yelled through the double doors of the dungeon. Thad wheeled the cart with the hanging rod to the door, using it to wheel himself around more quickly.

Twinge.

"Ah fuck!" Jack exclaimed as his neurological condition caught fire. "Babe…I might be headed for a storm."

Thad hobbled to his love with steel in his gaze. "And?"

"And? And…I might be headed offline. You know how this goes." Jack's disappointment grew because the air was already supercharged with raw sexual energy.

"I want to see this through," Thad added. "Would you be okay with that?" Thad entered Jack's personal space, showcasing the twist in his groin. "I don't want to stop."

"It's just that it's late, and the past few days have been…."

Unrelenting, Thad began undressing Jack. "You don't have to do anything… just be with me. Let me show you this." He pulled the small, burned-black ash box out of the cart.

Jack began to crumble and fade, making it hard to stand. There was a newfound immediacy to the moment. In each other's eyes, they could see the acknowledgment that Jack's health was worsening. His storms were far more frequent these days—this was their new normal. However, the beauty found in such a cherished moment, couldn't be denied. They had found, as Thad described it, Zenith's Peak. There were tears in their eyes as the storm finally began to sweep Jack off to its shores.

"Jack!" Thad yelled, reaching for his husband. Jack's legs buckled beneath him, and they were both on the floor within seconds. "I want to do this," Thad said, holding and rocking Jack's body.

"Me, too," Jack muttered quickly. They were running out of time. "You sure?"

"Let's go—no rules, just what feels right. I can still be in the moment with you as I'm able. I can still kinda hear you." He paused, taking stock of his body and senses. "I can't always completely comprehend you. Voices are usually muffled but audible."

Thad opened the smudge box, swabbed his thumb, and then crossed Jack's forehead. Jack's eyes fluttered. His spine contracted in an S, the slither of a snake on the floor. He exhaled loudly as his ribcage contracted, and he stared at the ceiling. Jack slowly untethered from life. Then, like falling out of an airplane, it began…

Jack fell faster and faster. He braced for impact while hearing in the background, "What I [unintelligible] you tonight is [unintelligible] clarify [unintelligible] your mind a few things."

CRASH!!! He felt the first impact against a solid surface. Jack's body heaved with the sensation. His writhing body was immersed in a fit of the mind.

Thad's voice rang on in the background. "…level in [unintelligible] minds. Others [unintelligible] has to be [unintelligible] [unintelligible] [unintelligible]. They [unintelligible] [unintelligible]…."

Jack gasped for air in the murk. He could tell his body back on earth was being fucked—hard. The back and forth of being rammed from behind increased as his mind sloshed. The sensation grew as stimuli became even more intense and the sound and light painful. The shards of noise pierced his mind like daggers. Lights flashed as Thad's body banged against his harder and faster.

"…the, as you [unintelligible] Advanced Class [unintelligible] [unintelligible] [unintelligible]. You know [unintelligible] truth."

Jack fell through more layers and then recaptured his breathing. It had to start there first. It had to. He slowed himself, tethering to known and tangible objects.

"Why Rosalyn?" Jack heard his husband ask, then continued. "[unintelligible] Other side. Shaman [unintelligible] [unintelligible]. Duality."

None of it made sense to Jack's mind. The scant bits of information he could glean were like confetti in a hurricane. He gave in and let go.

"[unintelligible] [unintelligible] Anam Cara… [unintelligible]. Singularity."

The slap of Thad on him was both fantastic and terrifying.

"Do you understand? [unintelligible] hear me?" His body rocking faster now, and in the distance he heard a distinct click from the center of his universe. His brain sizzled, hitting red hot as its center fizzed. He fell farther into the twister of neurological chaos.

"Beloved… [unintelligible]. Ethers to know [unintelligible] [unintelligible]. Was how we [unintelligible] [unintelligible] your mind. It's from [unintelligible] [unintelligible] [unintelligible]."

Blank. Jack's mind disconnected. This was always the scariest part—the part without stimuli for him to attach. All-encompassing white—bright white air—surrounded him. It's not as frightening when you can't see them, Jack involuntarily remembered.

"You [unintelligible] mine." The sloshing of his body on the floor was a frayed mop undone—useless. Thad's voice progressively became louder. "[unintelligible] [UNINTELLIGIBLE] [UNINTELLIGIBLE]. Forever! Unbreakable! [UNINTELLIGIBLE]." Jack felt himself being flipped over. He was floating. He wasn't sure where he was, but then he changed his point of view and hovered over his own body, where he saw Thad complete the kink that was them. His husband was fucking the hell out of Jack's lifeless body, and all he could do was watch with a smile. Jack would always passionately remember this moment, because it showed Thad's commitment to their weirdness, even when not required.

Jack then realized that outside his body, he could hear Thad perfectly. It wasn't choppy or distant or distorted, like it had been when he occupied himself. He listened.

"… forever with the Anam Cara," rang clear in his ear. "This is what awaits us, Jack, just there on the other side. But we must prepare you for Rosalyn. She holds the key for us both. Please—just be open to what she has to show you. We all know we're running out of time."

Jack then felt Thad hit him. SMACK! Then again. SMACK! Repeatedly—just like he liked—forcing him back into his body where he could at last, taste his own blood. It was ecstasy, and from the center of the storm where Jack lived, it taught him. It taught him about inhabiting chosen places and pleasure, and pain. But most importantly, it taught him how two people could take themselves to the edge of humanity just to see, what the fuck was there.

RAPIER DOWN

As January and February drew to a close, it was undeniable—Jack's health was failing. When he could manage, he'd head out to the back of the property for a cold morning moment to sketch, doodle, think, and figure.

There was too much to deal with to try and be calm. A newfound fire of desperation set in, found in swirls and mists of mysterious Thad. All of his unknown ways both fascinated Jack, and scared him. Often, when he witnessed the edges of worlds his lover would visit, he'd wonder what was there.

March approached, and Jack began to see the value of the lessons that Thad was feeding him. They didn't have long before Rosalyn would arrive. However, Jack was no beginner to Thad's spirit practices, he simply wasn't aware that what he had been doing had a name. A big name—one that could forge a journey for one, that would take lifetimes to best. For Jack, his big breakthrough came exactly when it always does—when all hope is lost—when you finally stop fighting or trying. And it was at this intersection, of Jack losing both his body and his future, that he discovered, he was also losing his mind.

"Okay…" Thad led as they found their way to their prayer mats early one late February morning. Jack, as always, was slow to be productive, but quick to offer drama.

Jack moaned. "Why?"

"Babe. C'mon… You've been so close. Let's see what we can do today to affect the world, versus it affecting you. That's where you'll find your personal power." They stopped to look into each other's worlds. "Choose everything as a yes. Even the awful. Even the unforgivable."

"The unforgivable…? Like the earliness of this chat?" They laughed.

"C'mon mate. Try."

"Okay…"

They centered on their mats and then fell into themselves, abandoning the physical for the beyond-the-physical. Within minutes Thad had them ambling down a trail behind the veil.

"What's true for you here Jack?" Thad asked quietly. "What can you hear here? What whispers on the wind are forming themselves into messaging? Where are you finding connection?" Several minutes went by. "Is there a guide here for you?"

With time, Thad led Jack further and further down the well-worn path found behind the veil, and gave him names of all the places that he had explored. The ancestral lineage, the Cave of Cats, the real yet unseen, the portals of possibility and the forward remembering…

Hours later, Jack reentered the home from his morning tree-time.

"How's the writing coming along?" Thad asked warmly as the scent of baked items met Jack at the door. "Anything we spoke of jumping you into action or understanding?"

"Dunno… Sometimes, like this morning… I can't seem to find the jumping-off point. Where do you focus when you first start telling a story?"

"Oh! You're thinking about your book? Well, first off, are you telling *a* story or are you telling *your* story?"

"What?" Jack found himself metaphorically on his heels. Thad reached for Jack and pulled him in for a hug.

"Listen, mate. I get you want to do this your way… but maybe you can lean on my experience to at least find the entrée to your message."

"I'm too scattered, aren't I?"

Thad laughed. "It's not your strongest asset." Jack's moonbeams hit Thad's sunshine as they twisted and wrestled with the matter at hand.

"I'm such a failure."

"Jack, love, don't do that. This is new to you. Maybe we can sit down together and outline what you want to say. Then with your writing, all you have to do is connect the dots."

"No. I need to figure this out on my own."

"It's just—" Thad tried.

"No," Jack repeated. "But I'll meet you halfway, and we can talk about a few things."

"Okay."

"What are ways to tell a story? What are my options?"

They made their way to the breakfast nook. "Well, you can tell it from an outside perspective or your point of view."

Jack blanked. "Meaning?" His lack of formal education gnawed at his insides.

Thad took Jack's hands. "The point of view in your story is where to begin. Are you the narrator or someone else?"

"Well, neither."

"Good. That's a start. Who's telling the story?"

The room was silent for a moment while Jack found his trailhead. "I was thinking it could be told from my higher mind."

"As in who?"

"As in the observer."

"So… Your mind, but not you—the one in your mind who observes Jack? Is that who's telling your story?"

Finally, Jack's blue mood gave way to pink. "Bingo!" And with that, the connection took. Jack excused himself from the table and all but ran to his computer. He fired it up while a known buzz in his fingers again caught.

He blanked his mind and began to write his story as told to him by his observer, the one in his head who sees without attachment. He remembered back to when his mind first awakened… He started typing…

Standing in the employee parking lot of Plexus Foods, Jack exhaled into the dark Canadian heavens. "I don't get it." He just had the worst day, and he simply didn't see the point of the exercise anymore. He focused on the North Star, his star. "How I wonder what you are—because how can you expect me to do this world right when I arrive to it so…?" Before he finished his thought, his boss's word "ineffective" rang in his working ear. "How?" Jack shook his head for answers. "How does any of this make sense? I thought.…"

He grabbed a joint from his bag and lit it while still mad-wondering at the Gods. "I thought you were supposed to be, you know, conspiring for my success or some bullshit." Jack paused and closed his eyes again, dragging hard then exhaling smoke. "Em told me that. She knows about these things even if she.…" Jack didn't want to think about it further, so he stopped and refocused on the night's horizon. "I thought in this place we were supposed to learn how to be kind and walk each other home, because that's what I learned in your god damned church!" He shouted heavenward. "Well fuck your god!"

Jack stopped writing and stood. He had done it. He broke through and found the beginning of his story.

DWINDLED

It was a mid-March morning when, Jack Daw crowed, "Just two weeks until Rosalyn is here!"

"You ready for her?" Thad laughed.

Jack arranged his face to reflect the statement, "No, baby cakes. The question is, is she ready for me?" He then struck one of his dumbest modeling poses, which always made Thad laugh.

"Mate, ain't no one ready for that." He pulled in close. "Except me."

Twinge.

"God damn it!" Jack yelled, deflating in spirit. "Babe. I think I need to go lie down."

"You okay?"

"Just the usual. It was so much easier when I could count on mornings being free of this shit. Gah, I hate my life."

Thad gave Jack a little warm shake. "Hey, don't do that. Remember what we talked about." But it was too late. Jack was already well down the rabbit hole of despair. "Come." Thad stood, and they walked shoulder to shoulder down the hall to their bedroom to take care of life.

Twinge. Jack's right hand contracted and cramped as they got themselves arranged. They lay in bed, and in their usual way, Thad grabbed on and went for the ride.

Twinge. Jack's neck began to curl. They breathed.

Twinge. Next, his spine and ribcage began the dance of the dystonic storm, only this time, his dance partner wasn't raw energy. It was his husband, who held on and spooned him.

Thad breathed slowly and softly, holding Jack as he slipped beneath the surface of his mind, but no one could have predicted that it would be twenty-four hours before he returned.

When he awoke, a nurse was tending to him.

"Welcome back," the male nurse said brightly.

Jack took in his surroundings, disoriented and woozy. "What happened?"

"Well, it seems you wouldn't come back this time without a little help." Thad entered the room to sit next to Jack, his face relaxing with relief.

"Mate…Jack, love." Thad kissed Jack generously. "I'm going to cancel my trip.

"The hell you are," Jack said flatly. "You know how much I've been looking forward to spending time with Rosalyn."

"Ya, but you're just….Maybe now isn't the time, given your need for increased care."

"No." Jack resisted the cage presented to his mind. "We always said we'd live fully, despite our crosses to bear. You said that. That's your case and position on life, not mine, so you're not going back on that now."

An odd silence hung between them, balanced on the fulcrum of fear and trust.

Thad seemed to be conferencing with himself before he replied, "Okay."

The following two weeks wander-mashed into more of the same. Jack did his best but flailed physically. However, when he was good, he could catch fire. There was this sense within him, of taking what Thad had shown him in their morning meditation sessions, and doubling it, then tripling it—no rules, truly flying free. Thad's words echoed in his mind. *Let's see what we can do today to affect the world, versus it affecting you. That's where you'll find your personal power.* Jack tried to reach for that truth, but often it simply seemed too big of a reach—and yet, he began to see the first edges of change within himself there. Change that dropped the heavy. Change that began to feel light. And oddly, it was this change, in a confluence of horrific events where the finish line of one's life is in sight, that Jack found bliss. He began each morning steeped in gratitude for another day, another chance to breathe and be with his love to explore the density of this god-forsaken world.

RISE

With Thad gone, Nancy announced Rosalyn's arrival as she pulled up to the driveway. Jack internally clapped while grabbing for his wheelchair and heading for the front door. Today, his lower half was pretty much offline, yet he remained grateful for what he had.

More than anything these days, the blessings of such gifts outshone all else. Jack bounced a beam of gratitude off the beautiful home's high ceiling as he opened the front door to greet Rosalyn in the warming spring sunshine.

"Oh my gosh," Jack said as he clapped electric shards of purple bright. "I have been so excited to see you again."

Rosalyn, with her signature wispy grey hair pulled into a bun on the top of her head, bent to hug Jack in his chair. She smelled of patchouli and rose water. "You look wonderful, my friend. You are simply glowing." She stepped back taking in his visage. "You look…" She fake-turned her head to see if anyone was listening and then continued in a loud whisper, "Dare I say happy?"

Jack caught the act and loudly whispered back, "I'll allow it."

Rosalyn then stood fully and confirmed aloud, "Happy!" They both burst out laughing, taking in the waves of refresh.

"I know!" Jack exclaimed. "Weird, right?!"

"SO WEIRD!" Rosalyn said to the heavens, while the trails of fabrics that were her, swirled with the motion.

"Come in. Come in," Jack said as Nancy snuck past him to help Rosalyn into the house. Jack wanted to help but soon realized his best course would be to sideline himself and his wheelchair, and not become a stumbling block.

Nancy and Rosalyn introduced themselves, and they arranged a quick tour.

"Would you like to unpack?" Nancy asked once they gathered back in the front foyer.

"Oh, that won't be necessary." Her response caught the other two off guard.

Jack hesitated, unsure of what was happening because of Rosalyn's very queer expression. The silence hung in the air while she, looking like your best friend's grandma, became ever more devilish with each passing second.

"Might I recommend something else, young man?" She stooped, coming face to face with him. "How about you and me beat a path down dockside?" She smirked then winked at Jack's register.

"Uh," he stumped and stammered.

"Uh nothing, go get your things." She pointed back toward Jack's room.

"But," Jack started, while his thoughts limited his access to options.

Nancy stepped in. "He's not really in a condition to leave."

Rosalyn rose to her full height of 5' 3" and said with such authority that even the dog's butthole shrank, "I've got this."

She definitely wasn't a woman to be taken lightly, and in this swirl, Jack remembered who Rosalyn was to Thad. She had been one of his teachers and mentors, and she was a force. Jack slyly smiled while Rosalyn continued facing him directly.

"You want to continue your isolation here? Or we could spend a few nights on a fabulous houseboat I rented for the weekend. The choice is yours."

Jack did a spit-take, despite not currently drinking anything. He found her directness both assaulting and fabulous. *God, I love her.* Jack thought. "I'll go pack."

Nancy frowned but didn't continue to argue. "I could use the rest," she said under her breath as she left the room.

Jack packed his best yachting outfits, along with….

"Along with…." Jack heard from behind him. He had forgotten Rosalyn could read thoughts. He wheeled around. "Along with a few other things," she continued, piquing Jack's curiosity.

"Such as," Jack tried to manage, but before he could finish the sentence, Rosalyn took control of his wheelchair and Broom Hilda'd him down the hall. He burst out laughing. Joy barked merrily, joining the action as they all whisked toward the foyer with terrific speed.

"Woo!" Jack yelled as they tore down the hall.

"Such as," Rosalyn repeated, turning them into the kitchen and crossing the room to the pantry.

Holy shit. Jack thought. *Is this what I think it is?* She hit the elevator button, and in they went. Jack noted how well she somehow knew the house, and the basement!

"So…," Jack said as casually as possible as the elevator began its descent. However, he realized how terribly he failed as a smile crossed Rosalyn's cheeks.

"Won't hurt a bit." She winked and then pushed Jack's chair out into the basement floor, where she parked him and forged on to the black cabinets. Jack watched her open chests and boxes to pick at items before tucking them into her purse.

Within four minutes, they returned to the elevator facing the mirrored doors when Rosalyn dropped his obsidian King's crown on his head. Jack laughed. "You'll be needing this." Her expression both delighted and terrified him.

They collected Jack's luggage and piled them into the back of a town car taxi, that was waiting out front. Once the luggage and wheelchair were put in the back of the vehicle, Rosalyn had them seated in the back then gave the address of their destination to the driver.

Off they went, and Jack was surprised at how good it felt to get out of the house and escape the vibrations of certain rooms that still haunted him.

"Where are we going?" Jack asked, embodying an undone blather of mixed emotions, while wringing his hands.

Rosalyn looked at him tersely. "What is wrong with you?"

Jack deflated. "Why?"

"It's like you've been on planet earth for four seconds." She stared into Jack's still-panicked heart. Jack blinked rapidly. She pulled in closer to Jack. "Right now… What are you doing?"

Jack blankety-blanked on his words mid-stammer. "Do…?" He finally eked out, making Rosalyn put the back of her hand to Jack's forehead as if checking his temperature.

"Check in with yourself right now, child."

Jack did so very briefly, which was needed given the sheer screaming-mimi effect of the atoms animating his, now frenetic, being.

"Oh," Jack said while doing his best to rearrange his energy.

"To be honest, Jack, I want to show you some things… I think there are some things you need to see for yourself, but this will <u>not</u> work if you're undone and sliding off to other planes."

Jack acted cool, but internally he was still fairly chaotic. Rosalyn held out a flat palm toward Jack. "Take my hand. Do this." Jack slowly put his palm into hers. "You're here…" She blasted frenetic energy into Jack, who warbled and bug-eyed. "And I need you here." Jack then felt calm, soothing vibes pulse through him.

"Oh," Jack noted, her meaning clear. She fascinated him. Her unique ability was to wield force over energy as if she merely waved hello.

Rosalyn piled herself into a dump of scarves and looked out the window again. "Are you paying attention, Jack?" The car meandered to the coastline, and Jack couldn't garner a response to her question.

"Your specific soul lives in a minefield. That's just simple fact. So how does one navigate crossing such a place?"

"Carefully?" Jack offered but then continued his silent vigil only to be slap-prompted by the unamused elder.

"Child, who has been teaching you?"

He searched for his best answer. "I guess I have—sometimes Thad."

"Oh." She was clearly unimpressed as she chased a tissue around the inside of her purse. "Well, that explains a lot."

Rosalyn's response highly amused Jack, but there was also a dash of uncertainty about where this was headed. Jack held tremendous respect for Rosalyn—respect that bordered on making him very, very nervous. His social anxiety grew as he realized the gig was up. He was caught.

Faker! his innards punched at him. Jack quickly disconnected from his fear portal and re-centered himself in the present.

Meeting the moment, he glanced over at Rosalyn. She waved a tissue to God, clearly witnessing Jack's chosen energy shift. "At least it's a start. Fine. We're not starting from scratch." She then doubled down with, "I can work with that, and if you have concerns about access to medical care, sweetie, I have it covered." She put a hand on Jack's shoulder. "Our houseboat is close to a water-accessed hospital dock. Plus, I have people we can call, depending on what happens." She paused, as if choosing her next words carefully. "However, let's abandon the concept of unseen fear, Jack. Let's make smart, wise decisions and yet dare greatly. Live on the edge." She grabbed his hand and shook it with encouragement.

Jack blushed. He felt called out.

They arrived at the water's wharf where a two-man crew met them. "This is Jose and Mike," Rosalyn said, making the introductions.

They made their way down to the boat and carted the lot on board the small two-story barge.

"The main floor is all one level, so if you need to wheel around, you should be good. I checked on that." She patted Jack as she wheeled him to his room. "The crew is up, and we're down here. Let them do the stairs, I figure. You need to lay down for a bit or…?" She again placed the back of her hand to his forehead. "Nah, you're good."

She scurried Jack's belongings, and within minutes, he was properly arranged and enjoying the sea-view. The vessel shifted as it unmoored, and their voyage commenced.

TIDAL

"Come." Rosalyn grabbed Jack's hands and pulled his wheels toward the stern. "We have a sitting area here to watch the sunset. Wine?"

Jack laughed and parked himself on a banquet of cushions. "If you insist," he said, loving the beginning of their grand adventure.

Rosalyn soon returned to the table with two very healthy pours. The boat slowly coasted on, the amble of the vessel in step with Jack's mood, echoed in the soft sprays of surf and the beaming rays of the late afternoon sun on the water. Jack closed his eyes and breathed it all in, holding the moment in his mind.

With his eyes still closed to God, Jack said, "There's been something on my mind." Rosalyn, mid-sip, nodded for him to go on. He opened his eyes and looked candidly into hers. "Like, this thing you do, you know, directing energy and…." He silently mimed the remaining words with broad sweeping arms.

Rosalyn chuckled. Her voice betrayed that she found this show of Jack a total delight. "You are a bucket of half-washed socks at best, yet somehow, one can't help but love you for it. What is it?"

"Well…" Jack stopped talking.

"You want to know if I can make you well?" she finally asked.

Jack burst to life. "Yes! Can you?" His mind was on board with another exorcism, faith healing, or whatever her version was.

Rosalyn laughed. "Oh, child." She patted the seat next to her. "Only you are powerful enough to do that. Come, back to back. Sit. Match me." She turned to face the side of the ship on the extended bench, legs tucked neatly under her. Jack scrambled ungracefully to land his spine against hers.

"Like—?" he tried, only to be cut off by Rosalyn.

"Like, shut up!" she said with power in her voice. However, this time, the aim was clearly humor. They both laughed. "Settle yourself," she clarified. They hummed silently into the ocean air.

Without direction, Jack matched her vibe. She went silent—as did Jack—but he noted that while they were vocally silent, the humming in the background somehow continued.

Jack hadn't expected that. He listened to it more closely, searching. What was it made ov? What was its essence? What was its root composition? He didn't know but remained curious, allowing its truth to be shown to him.

Still. Nothing.

A few minutes passed, and Jack became frustrated with the lack of answers. No new information arrived, and for the life of him, he couldn't place the origins of the humming resonance.

"*It's a sound?*" Jack inquired silently.

"n o," his gut replied.

"*Is it a feeling?*" But he knew it wasn't as soon as the question formulated.

"n o."

Next, Jack flipped up for a closer inspection. The chatter of his mind fell away, and he instantly transported to the field of clarity—the observation deck of his mind.

He exhaled thinking, *Ah, the expanse of the air here.*

"It's like you can breathe again," Rosalyn put into his mind.

Hearing this, Jack screamed, "VooDoo!" and burst out of his meditative state, where he was met by Rosalyn, who slowly turned, aghast.

"For serious, son?" she said without emotion, making Jack laugh out of sheer embarrassment.

"I'm so sorry. I sometimes get lost in the moment."

Rosalyn put her feet on the floor, facing the front of the ship. Jack maneuvered his dead legs to approximate a similar position.

"That was impressive, Jack." Rosalyn looked straight ahead.

"What?" he questioned.

"What you did there. You saw a new thing and got curious about it. You tried to dissect it, but when no reliable conclusion came, you backed away to see if it would come to you. Where did you learn that?"

He considered his response. "I'm not sure..." He thought more while Rosalyn allowed him the chase. "I guess sometimes I get curious about the origins of things."

"And what have you discovered?" she asked.

Jack cast off the expected and searched for his best truth. "I have discovered that there are layers to things, you know." He faced the other side of the blue and orange sky. "The superficial or surface stuff is but a veneer, and the rest of everything is behind that."

"Like what? What's behind that?" she prompted.

"Like time." Jack searched as Rosalyn laughed in delight. "Like space, distance, or...."

"Or things separate?" Rosalyn offered, dropping the clue.

The question made Jack internally burst a pipe. "YES! Oh my God," Jack exclaimed energetically, the thrill of finally scratching the exact source of a pestering itch. "YES!" he repeated.

The collapse of him into a new truth was hysterical for Rosalyn, like watching a puppy bite his tail.

"How did you...?" Jack didn't finish the question because he had already found the answer. He knew she was reading his every move.

They sat and watched the sunset. The long rays of the north and its hours-long twilight changed everything around them minute by minute—a show neither one of them dared to miss.

"You haven't had much direction, have you?" Rosalyn prompted with a question that, weirdly, always made Jack feel emotional.

Gah, he told himself, displeased with his thick humanness.

"But you're doing it, Jack. You're changing the world."

Jack's belief in everything flatlined while trying to assess the words that hung like lies in the air.

"I'm what?" His disbelief was complete as Rosalyn took in Jack's sheer undoneness. "How?" eventually vacated Jack's untethered mouth.

She turned to face Jack. "Every flower that blooms on earth changes it."

"So what?" Jack laughed. "I just fruited?"

Rosalyn chuckled. "Only you, dear heart."

They regained themselves, watching the beautiful, shifting colors of the expansive sky.

"Let me ask you something." She paused before continuing. "How were you able to identify the observer with so little direction? How did you find that place?"

"I'm sorry I don't follow."

Rosalyn grabbed Jack's hand and punched deep into his being, the mental space of clarity free from the ick of ego and judgment. "This!"

As she uttered that single word, Jack's world exploded. Her energy suddenly encompassed everything for miles, and she single-handedly, in one utterance, laid waste to every other vibe or resonance that planet earth currently engaged in. She flat leveled all sound for miles. The cosmic sweep of silence was absolute and vast, and the hum left in its wake shocked Jack, not by what he heard or saw but by how she energetically charged his entire being. He completely buzzed anew.

What the fuck, Voodoo Lady? he thought to himself sheepishly, eyes wide. He settled as sound began to return.

Rosalyn simply watched him and sipped her wine. "Not bad. Except that last bit. Access to the silent mind that is free of chatter. On your own, you found clarity, the one who observes."

"Ya, ya… But God! Don't just like, you know, put that crazy energy in me like that. What the hell was that? You can just ask," Jack said, not knowing why he felt violated, like he wanted to turtle off and close up shop. "I can get there on my own," he pained while rubbing his arm where she had connected to his field.

"Ah. That's where he lives," she uttered to no one. "He's deep purple. Got it." Rosalyn stood to head for the access corridor. "Come. Rest before dinner." She pointed toward his room and turned, entering hers.

An hour later, Rosalyn roused Jack. "Hey," she said softly, rocking him on his bed.

"Bleh," Jack mumbled with one-eye in her direction. She laughed.

"Dinner is being served soon." She left Jack to pull himself together.

Jack sat up to assess the capabilities in his now, not-working legs. Weirdly, they were still not functioning, and it had been a week. He side-stepped the terror and reached for his wheelchair.

C'mon fucknut, Jack told himself as his "I-got-this" attitude notably dimmed from wear. He managed a change of shirts and rearranged his hair into a more distinct bedhead look. "Let's do this!" He glided toward the main dining area.

"Ah," Rosalyn watered. "Don't you look nice." The motherly goodness of the woman delighted and warmed a space in Jack. He smiled and then high-saluted, wheelie style. Rosalyn clapped at the effort. "Come," she directed. "Sit. Sit." Rosalyn tucked Jack under the table that was already bustling with objects, and bottles and such.

"Did you cook?" Jack asked.

Rosalyn cut a look. "Baby." She paused and then clarified, "I am on vacation just as much as anyone else here." She then caught the crew in a glance. "Except you two. We need you two to, you know…." She took a slug of wine. "…Do manly stuff." Jack did not expect this and once again found himself spit-taking without water.

Just then, a water taxi pulled up next to their boat, and anchored in the bay. "Yes." Rosalyn encouraged the crew to action. "Can you…?" Her waving arms seemed to help them understand the charge.

Within a minute, Jose and Mike returned with boxes of food.

"Voila!" Rosalyn pointed to the boxes. "Dinner." She turned to the crew members. "Sit. You won't be taking yours to your room just yet. We need yuz to sit here and look cute." She winked at Jack.

"Gracias," Jose said. "You're very kind." Jack hadn't noted previously that Jose's first language wasn't English, but then again, they had only said "hello" to one another on the way in.

"Were you born in Canada?" Jack asked Jose.

"Nah," Jose replied. "Tijuana." He looked around quickly. "But I like it better here now."

"You didn't want to try the USA? Wasn't it easier?" Jack asked.

Jose laughed. "We share the same drunk neighbor. Do I need to explain?" Everyone chuckled.

"Gotcha." Jack pointed and winked. "Say no more."

They all enjoyed each other's company, and as night gained to full, Jack slid downhill mentally. The constant rocking unmoored him, plus alcohol always added challenges. Rosalyn was the first to catch onto his shift.

"Jack, sweetie. How are you doing?" she asked as the ship bounced lightly in the new Canadian night.

Jack turned and said, "Choo. Key."

Fuck! Jack thought. The weirdness of the sensation was unexplainable. He couldn't understand how he could think in English, yet only gibberish came out when he tried to verbalize it.

"Excellent." Rosalyn stood. "Boys? Can we get Jack en haut?" She pointed to the second floor. "There's a few things that I need Jack to see—best he be closer to God." They were soon a muddle of upward direction, chasing figures and hidden places.

LAX

Jack hadn't been upstairs before and was surprised at how chic it was. There were two little rooms on the front side and a reasonably spacious common area deck sternward. It was sparsely furnished with a picnic table and a few chairs, then a blue and white striped rug to formalize the space.

Sweet, Jack thought.

"Come!" Rosalyn directed. "Put him on there." Mike and Jose attempted to seat Jack at the table, at which point they were immediately backhanded by a grandmotherly slap. "No, no," she said under her breath to the men. "I said ON the bloody table."

Her head shaking eventually brought her close to Jack's face, cradled between the crew members' hefty chests. "Comfy, dear?" She asked. Jack smirked in response. "Can you nod, love?" He did. "Well, at least we have that." She turned to the tabletop and back. "Can you sit up?" Jack shrugged slightly—it was clear his mind was sliding.

The men helped him into a seated position on the tabletop. He felt like a weird piece of art being appraised. Jack protested in gibberish, his verbal bitching accompanied by several very pointed and aggressive gesticulations. They all awoke to the reality of the situation and stepped in quickly to help the mad-directing Jack.

"Now, now," Rosalyn shooed the men. She then did a quick redirect to Jack, whispering. "Shooing men. Gah." She gave Jack a wink. "We'll cover this too."

Shoeing men? he thought, looking at their feet.

Eventually, Rosalyn and Jack sat spine to spine. This time, though, they were table-topside under the night's newly found billion-star broadcast. It was simply breathtaking. The humble grace of the green Northern Lights danced as the splash and lap of waves from afar hit gently against the boat's solid broadside, a rocking lullaby from the sea that set the mood for a night filled with possibilities.

Rosalyn adjusted herself onto a cushion so the back of their skulls could meet more evenly. "Nod, Jack." Her tone was authoritative. "What can you do? What do you know?"

Jack quickened in the night, his nervousness growing.

"Jack!" Rosalyn punctured into him. "Cease." He couldn't comprehend her words. "Jack, cease."

His anxiety spiraled.

"God damn it, child." Rosalyn flipped around and kneeled behind Jack, pushing her tummy into his spine, holding his head with one palm on his forehead, the other an exact opposite match. "JACK," she threw into him. "CEASE! Why are you failing to act?"

It was her! Rosalyn made him nervous. He grabbed at its truth and then flipped up to the observation deck to the mind for clarity.

Calm air....

They both returned to normal breathing. "You were damn near going to make me level you up without your permission again." It was clear she didn't have time for games. "I thought you said you didn't care for that?"

Jack murmured through half-working lips. Still in the attack, processing what was happening kept tripping him up.

Rosalyn rearranged them into a totem pole of faces. Behind him, she palmed his mind, settling it into her insight. She blanked to the source and then opened, asking, "What can you do? What do you know? Show me."

Jack tried again to achieve a common arrangement of himself, but the gig was up. Rosalyn, without opening an eye, smacked his head. "Stop that." She repositioned slightly. "Beginners," she mumbled. She again erected them to a focus. "Child," she said under her breath. "Be who you are... and yes! That means to be where you are on all levels, on all days. Why do you fight this concept so? You are as you're supposed to be. See it." She embraced and rocked him, and they went in for another try.

This time, Jack let go and simply went with the momentary mumble-mush that was him, scars and all, which, while in a neurological attack, was his flow and his truth.

"There we are," Rosalyn assured as the tension diminished. "That's you being you. Because if that were me and I was your age again, I would enjoy the hell out of it."

Jack smiled a flop of lips.

"Trust," Rosalyn said. Jack noted the ping of the thing, recognizing the hours of work he had done around the concept of the word she just uttered. "Trust." She repeated. He had been working on understanding its vibration.

Trust, Jack thought.

"There it is," Rosalyn said as they simmered in flow. "Keep yourself there." The salty air was calming to Jack's mind…

He allowed himself to be as he was. *Trust…. Why is that so…?*

"Mighty?" Rosalyn finished, to which Jack's energy affirmed. "We'll get there. Come now, Jack. Let's go again."

The swim of them hit repeat. She pulled Jack into totem pole position, to face the truth of the sea. She straightened them up.

"What do you know? Jack, can you show me? Inhabit it so I may know it too." She stirred him, holding tight. "Show me what you are ov. Go! I will meet you there," she encouraged. "And Jack?" He did his best to look at her. "Trust." She then retook his face to oppose it, to link with Jack's truth and feel his vibe and throttle. "GO!" she yelled smiling, flinging his unmoored mind into deep space.

As he was launched deep behind the veil, the reel of Jack was on, and he took off like cracking white lightning.

Ready, Voodoo Lady? He cracker-jacked smartly, making Rosalyn laugh.

Jack blasted off, wanting to impress her—he knew this place. Mid-mind tumble, he righted himself to a float then searched the backside of his mind. He searched for levers and lenses as he flung himself inward into options, switching out his five senses to their heightened twenty-five viewpoints.

Next, he journeyed out his tendrils to set them to sail as he expanded them again, furthering their reach to yet further posts. He unwound his seeking charges through layer after layer, chasing far distant winds with feelers of knowing.

"Woo-hoo!" Rosalyn screamed mid-mix of their swirl. The ride was intoxicating, with the wilds of youth. She again centered to grab Jack's energetic tailcoats and shored them up as the student dove further into his journeying state—the conscious portal of shamans, and gods.

His heightened state was like a peacock, a massive far-flung expression of bold and bright. He grabbed at the posts for more tethers, knows, and gets. He unfurled feelers for senses that captured soft whispers. He spidered and tethered them to posts and balustrades found in far-off balconies, bridges, and terraces found in other worlds. He worked as quickly as possible, setting up a network of feelers that would radio knowledge to his networking ear, where he saw the universe's expanse without relying on his eyes. He needed vision, not sight.

Once the sails were set, he blanked to the stormy beach on the far side of his mind and grabbed for it. Rosalyn screamed with the adventure, obviously not a ride she thought this young man was capable of.

Jack arrived then ran down the moonlit beach on the far side of his mind, screaming into Toby's cave. "YA!!!!" He ran farther on the surf and blasted the night sky hues from black to purple to rose.

Next, he dove into the icy water, where his demon hellcat lived, and allowed himself to slip through its bottom. Jack searched for a current to gentle him onto the Isle of Congress. "WOO-HOO!" he yelled, arriving at its shore. He stood, waiting for Rosalyn with a shit-eating grin.

Rosalyn soon arrived. "Okay, I'm impressed!"

Then Jack strode toward the war-torn office building and stepped inside to wait for his teacher at the now familiar receptionist's desk. Once again, the teacher arrived to find Jack's proud puss.

"Oh, Rosalyn, dear!" The receptionist said, clamoring as they bowed and kissed over the desk. "It's been so long." She turned to Jack and sized him up and down. "Is the stray yours?"

Jack's mouth opened in shock. *Stray?!* he thought.

"Yes, Lottie. Nice to see you," Rosalyn said over her shoulder. "Jack, nice trick, but let's let the nice people get their work done. Shall we?" She ushered Jack back into the field of shifting consciousness that gassed, clumped, gathered, and fell like a million peeping peers from judgmental eyes.

Fine, Jack thought to himself, feeling his competitive nature grow.

"You can't be serious," Rosalyn said from behind him.

Damn it! Jack thought, feeling caught yet again. He hated that she could read him so plainly. "Fine," Jack said and purposefully punched fear into himself to reach turf-side.

He opened his eyes once back on the ship's deck, breathing in the night air. *And Voodoo Lady, Jesus, what are you made of?*

Rosalyn quickly returned and slapped him upside the head. "Voodoo Lady?! Really?"

Jack tried to speak, but English words failed to form in his brain. He settled and allowed himself to refocus.

"Is there more?" Rosalyn finally asked flatly.

Jack grinned and nodded.

"Okay, then." She retook them into a mast at the edge of the conscious abyss. "Let's see what you have, child. Let's see what you know. Again, go. GO!"

Jack tethered to the closest shore and zeroed in on a tree on the beach. He threw out his feelers to connect with it, to know it. It was the path of mycelium this time, the fiber optics of the conscious earth. Jack connected to it, felt it, and knew its presence.

He allowed the exchange between them as sentient beings—channel open, mind and might alight. He allowed the flow to recycle through them both equally. They pulsed with it, and Jack met the plant nation where it was. Their meeting power-filled microscopic paths that glowed and throbbed bioluminescence blue in the night.

Jack smiled with the reconnection. Their soothing beingness was the only vibration on earth that connected him to source in this manner. He flung himself out—to greet it, to know it. To drink in its resonance and learn it would allow him to reproduce and then be it. Jack was on the cusp of learning what great shamans know—that there wasn't anything he hadn't been. He simply needed to remember.

I am the altar, presented itself to Jack. He took it in with gladness and pocketed its presence for a later inspection. Then, Jack disconnected from the path to look into the heavens.

"Yes, child," Rosalyn said with a smile.

Jack's heart center warmed, remembering when his heart, his feminine divine, took him into her star-spangled matrices. He remembered slipping out of his body to meet himself anew and finally find his right-size truth. He remembered the resonance of the all-knowing in the beyond. He remembered it, and then he sang with it. His body rendered to slack as he forged on, chasing after its afters. They floated through deep space, allowing the enormity of what was, to be.

Without making a sound, Jack vibrationally sang, *Heaven.* He remembered the lights from beyond and its many-sided spaces, pockets, and curtains.

Curtains! Jack fired to delight as he adopted an all-encompassing nothing while finding the exact current moment. He didn't have a pad and pencil to track it, so he used his good ear to tack the precise now with sound, and in but a moment, there it was—the curtain of tinkers, the causal plane.

He found its edge and stepped behind it—a wrinkle in space filled with whirring electronics and far-distant blinking lights.

Jack stood on its vast edge and absorbed it, not as visual information but as an access point discovered by inputs found in his dark internal universe.

There was the presence here of vastness and expansion, including within himself. Everything moved at the speed of 73.3 km/s/Mpc—the expansion of all—and Jack felt like a growing giant. He stood in awe of the landscape's beauty. The air was so fresh, and he breathed in the cosmic sounds that swept across his broken face. Rosalyn soon arrived with him.

"It's beautiful," she said softly from behind. The night air blinked in both natural and electric-machine ways.

"It reminds me of being up on a mountain at night and looking down at a city in a valley that stretches on forever."

They silently drank in the view.

"Is there something you'd like to do while we're here, Jack?" She presented the question to the student, even though the truth of it would kill him.

"Maybe," he answered with an odd sadness.

"And what's that? What's your question for this place?"

"Can we fix me here?" Jack asked of the air before him.

The teacher pulled in close and hugged him. "Child, there is nothing to fix. You are as you are supposed to be."

Jack understood, catching her clarity. He was dying. It was his time, ready or not.

He allowed the reality of it to pass through him until he could breathe again. Jack understood the destructive force of complaint, and accepted what was, in an effort not to ruin the balance of their time together. He consciously chose not to inhabit a new potential sadness and the slime of it soon passed and then left.

"Excellent. Come," Rosalyn encouraged, squeezing his hand. "Let's not dwell. Too much yet to see, I imagine." She shook a charge of pep into them both. "Dear son!" she perked. "You are nothing short of amazing. I now understand what Thad went on about. Is there more?"

He nodded.

"Excellent." She winked with cheer. "Show me."

CETACEA

Jack thought about what to show Rosalyn next and landed on, "Sound!" He hummed tonally, then vibrationally. Rosalyn adopted the resonance of Jack, which sparked delight in her eyes.

"Sing, child," she said as she shored Jack's limp body at the top of the ship, his near unconscious state inconsequential to their gather and chase. Rosalyn popped a vibe into his fading way, which Jack took in and let settle into his guide's direction—the teacher leading by setting up energetic side rails and guide lights, but little else.

Jack resonated with a blessed hum as his alignment started to refuse his earthbound discord. He vibrationally rose as Rosalyn felt the sweep of its arc and encouraged it on.

"Yes, Jack!" she proffered. "There! Go there," she directed her charge deeper into the veil's secrets.

The sound vibrations flew at light speed, awakening all that was for miles. Slowly, the perk of those called, bubbled with the cognizance from the alert. From miles, they joined in howls, flicks, yips, and song. It was as if the air itself began to sing.

Rosalyn laughed and took in all the sounds of the frogs, raccoons, crabs, and trees. They joined Jack in his call that murmured and flowed, rejoicing only for the fact that they lived. Miles and miles it went, the harmony of earthly delight.

"Yes!" Rosalyn swept, directing her supervision. "Come." She grabbed Jack's energetic cottontail and punched them forward on a newfound course. "Hear it. Know it. Adopt it. Be it," she directed. "Never is nothing happening, child. GO! Search on… Release yourself."

Jack's ear searched the distance of his imagination. He heard it from his ears, then his mind, and then his soul. He heard the beat of a wing and knew its vibrational dark color. He heard the loons landing on far-flung lakes and knew of their texture. He heard the bullrushes and wild tobacco and knew of their taste.

"Chase bigger," the teacher prompted.

Chase bigger? he internally questioned.

"Oh, beginners." She swatted Jack. "No. No. Like this, child." Rosalyn gulped air like a toad and murmured anew while drum-rattling her energy and grabbing at Jack's skull to hold him aloft of his storm. "Ready?" As the point of connection on the ship, she took a twist of their everything, and in half a second, they met deep mid-ocean in a bubble beneath the sea. "Like this child. BIGGER!" Jack looked around in the bubble beneath the sea as Rosalyn pulled him in close to her and hit a stride he had never seen, experienced, or known. She revved in a start, holding back power until it fired to the max, and then it flew from her to the heavens as a beacon of light energy—the sea parting like one does to a Master.

"Hold on," she cried, the torrent around them shimmering and bubbling. Jack wasn't sure how they'd make it off the sea floor!

They re-engaged their tethers as Rosalyn continued the force that parted the sea and opens the sky—the place of childhood learning, curiosity, and care.

Jack's container quickly matched hers. *Got it!* He said internally as they blasted through the launch as Rosalyn's rocket shot on, peeling back the visible to reveal its organic truth. It was both atomic and subatomic. It was laws of reason, light years beyond current human consciousness.

From where their feet stood on the bottom of the sea, she showed Jack home, to which he wanted a map because this was his original wish. The map would show him how we walk each other home.

He did his best to view it—to see and know it—without collapsing. He took in its majesty and resonated with it in sacred ancestral kinship. Above them the sky somehow showing bright stars in the dimming light. A thing that cascaded in a collapsing matrix.

The parting of the sea held and began to settle as Jack looked around to see the earth anew—an earth with no veils or lies. His mind couldn't comprehend it, for it was beyond what he understood as form. Atoms danced in this place, all free, untethered, knowing no mind—and it was here he found atoms unobserved, carrying on in their multidimensional way.

Jack awed, trying to be one with the new know. But how does one grasp a place where darkness and light are one? There were no rules, where Jack could stand, learn, and be changed because the tribal hum he found in this space was currently unknown. It wasn't part of his universal song yet, so he learned it by heart while the space of the in-between opened wider and made itself known to his mind.

Jack gawked and figured. As he did so the beings who heard him offered their pop, song, and tenor. But it was more than a song. They were the sounds of life. Jack could finally hear while he inhabited this place.

"Holy fuck-wagons," Jack said with awe as Rosalyn laughed.

"What do you see?" she asked, prompting a lesson.

Looking around and trying to make sense of the undone matrix, Jack replied, "I don't know yet." His words were back.

"Would you like to?" Rosalyn offered.

"Yes, very much," Jack replied. *While I still can,* hit him like a drive-by. He side-stepped its ick to remain in curiosity. "What is this place?" he asked looking into the matrix as it continued to unravel before them.

"This exists not as a place but as a law," Rosalyn presented to him while checking on her word's take. Then her face changed showing that she saw it.

"There it is." She said clearly seeing that the student was finding the path.

They moved on as she closed the space. The ocean collapsed around them and united again as one.

Back on the ship, Jack opened his eyes to the moonlit waves crashing around the boat, wild torrents that swilled and swirled like monsters just beneath the sea. Eventually, it calmed as he did.

Jack exhaled and sat back into Rosalyn's arms, who was still holding him upright atop the balcony of the ship.

The old medicine doctor loosened her grip from around him and slowly regathered herself, checking if Jack could remain seated without her assistance.

Facing him, she twinkled with mischief and asked, "Now, what do you know?"

He thought about it, replaying his vibrational new-earth tone. "I don't know how to describe it."

"Perfect," Rosalyn said. "For it isn't a describable thing. That was bold of you to say that truth."

"What truth?" Jack asked.

The teacher rearranged her face. "It would have been easier for you to try and make something out of what you now hold, but you didn't. You named its truth to you as it was, not as it should be. With just this practice, one can have everything." She paused as if gathering her thoughts. "One cannot be a student to life if you think you know things."

Jack felt the vibe of the dystonic. "But you asked me what do I know? So how is it that knowing things is misaligned with learning?"

Rosalyn delighted in the sounds that fell from the mouth of babes. "Oh, dear child," she beamed. "You are a delight."

They silently sat beside one another, searching the horizon's new moon. Jack's curiosity overpowered the quiet calm. "How did you get there? Us into the ocean…" He searched his mind. "I know that finding the access point is the yang of it. And the rest is the yin—the allowing of what is—so there has to be a way in." Jack thought aloud. "Can you show me how you got there?"

"Where, child?" Rosalyn asked brightly. "Where did we go?"

Jack arrested himself to exhale and allow for new news. "I don't know yet. Was it a place we went or rather…. mind stuff…"

Rosalyn sat silently then spoke. "Saw anew."

The information befuddled Jack, who grabbed its utterance to seek clarity. "Sawanew?" He asked. "Is that…?"

Rosalyn laughed and clapped her hands.

"Algonquin?" He finally managed to feel stupid, not knowing why.

Rosalyn doubled over with laughter. "Oh, child," she said as a tear of joy found her cheek.

"What?" Jack asked, feeling weird. "Is that Cherokee or—"

Rosalyn quickly grabbed Jack's hands and asked directly, "Do I need to remove your remaining eye so you can finally see?"

Jack perked to life, stymied by fear. "But—" he tried.

Rosalyn put a finger to Jack's left side of his face. His "good side" served no real purpose or foresight. "This side of you serves no master." Her touch botoxed his functioning eye, putting out its light.

Realizing he was blind, Jack grew frantic and yelled, "Help!" His arms flailed, which Rosalyn caught to right. She punctured his everything to an immediate still.

"Ow," Jack once again complained.

"Quiet," she commanded. Silence fell in her wake as Jack rocked on with the ramble of the sea. He slowly remembered where he was and met the moment as he now saw it. It was only then that Jack finally accepted what the sea and seers see—true vision—waves beyond the visible. His third eye opened for the first time in his life.

"Yes," Rosalyn celebrated. "Check yourself."

Jack surrendered to the tabletop and reclaimed himself before a master who deserved silent listening and respect. Jack felt the humility of this crumbled rumble that now lived in his way. He silenced and stilled, knowing he would not disrespect the moment with his flail. He settled.

Rosalyn worked Jack into a child's pose on the table and checked in with his vibrational state, where she discovered him ready, arriving to know a new know, "Mitakuye Oyasın," she began. With a cosmic boom, "All my relations… COME." Jack's mind was unsure he could hold more as Rosalyn collected and opened, breached, and took down known laws. Her calling song took them from green to blue and beyond to the farthest flung darkest purple to the land of Jack's way, for on this Shamanic journey, it was time he met himself where he lived.

The medicine woman's song simmered and echoed, and once again, the sea churned a response. In Jack's blinded state, he told himself he was lost, which ultimately was the lesson to find one's way out of oneself. In the distance, Jack heard a song that sang back!

"Holy fuck!" Jack let escape, hearing that the new voice was guttural, often piercing, and massive. He recognized the call and trained himself to open and connect with nature, only this time without the blindness of sight. This time Jack knew the sound, and without his impairing vision, he was all ears.

"Listen," Rosalyn whispered to him, holding his head still. He realized there was more now ov him to listen from. He ran to his other openings for more information. He listened with his sense of touch to feel its sound. He listened with his sense of taste to imbue the song's matter. He listened with his sight and then finally blanked to clarity.

He recognized this song.

"Whales," Jack whispered, feeling them begin to arrive, their hale bouncing the boat in the waves like a toy.

LEAGUE

"Rosalyn!" Jack punch-clamored, not trusting the enormity of what was happening as the ship began to tilt, bargain, and list. "Please… I'm blind!"

"Interesting choice," she said while watching the student put enough emotional water into himself to drown.

"Sweetie," Rosalyn slapped Jack's face. "Honey…." She was still trying to get his attention. "Damn it, Jack!" He finally resurfaced with a gasp in a state of blind, frantic shock.

"Tadpoles," Rosalyn wondered aloud at him. "Jack?" She lightly slapped his face again. "You're not doing this well." He was still trying to right himself mentally as she continued with further directions. "Why are you letting your mind call the shots? Jack…." She slapped him more. "That's very stupid," she said, clocking the beginner's wallow of unchecked emotions. "So counterproductive," she muttered as Jack flailed and fought.

On it went, and with so little vision or clarity, Jack grasped at nothing. "I'm sorry," he clamored, desperately seeking known objects, even though the solution he sought couldn't be found in moments past, but finally, right in plain sight.

"Jack," Rosalyn said calmly. "I cannot do the work for you." Her words offered zero direction. She touched a calm into his undone way and waited for the settle.

In the distance, more roaming pods of enormous beasts began to churn and sing.

"Come," Rosalyn commanded to all who were not using eyes for sight. The whales sang as Jack finally stilled.

Hearing his teacher's call and her commencement command, Jack leaned into his training. He slowed and focused on the elder's meaning, his connection to self-honor, and then assumed the ask's mindset. Jack knew he was no longer in the beginner's class, so he followed his guide's charge. Wishes that become habits that become truths.

The call of "Come" was the command to level and then drop. However, this time, with no sight to begin to close off from, Jack dropped a layer further down than he previously knew existed. His deeper jumping-off point led him somewhere yet to be seen.

"Finally!" Rosalyn said to God. The beautiful awful of watching a child try and tie their shoes then cross the street on the first day of school, where struggle meets small victories that wander into traffic. They both exhaled as Jack assessed his new location—a location of tonal and vibrational command.

From behind the blind, he assessed the place. However, so many questions peppered Jack that it was paralyzing. His curiosity dial was set to max, as he unconsciously flipped into his higher mind for a clearer, quieter electronic view.

Jack paused, recalling his lesson around this. When in the presence of something not yet understood, pause, inquire, then open, and allow. The value of the exercise is incalculable—the osmosis of still and the exchange of only being present. Jack opened his chest to its new tonal reality and allowed himself to be known by it and it by him, just like he had done with a Great White Wolf so many days ago.

A deeper deep, Jack knew anew as his thoughts were also available here in non-earthbound auditory information. Rosalyn laughed, hearing him reverberate from that place turf-side. *Ha!* Jack internally laughed into the deeper deep. Hearing the laugh's echoes, he caught a curious

Hello! He smiled as distant salutations went further flung into space. *Hello… Hello… Hello…* sound waves carried and cried.

But then there was a response! He heard a gargantuan burp and squeal from the deep. Jack closed in for a closer inspection.

Why can I understand this? Jack didn't have a way to describe what he suddenly knew. He felt Rosalyn enter the space. He searched for a clue. *Why did I comprehend the meaning behind that noise?* He asked with itchy innards. The discomfort of a new understanding this big made him feel feeble and tiny, like this information would crush him and short-circuit his mind.

Rosalyn touched Jack's way back to calm. "Breathe." They both slowed to check Jack for okayness. He smiled. "Jack," she began. "When we look at words through the lens of universal truth, no translation is needed because they all sound the same." Jack didn't understand, which was clarified by his teacher. "Ah. There he is," she said, then zeroed in "Do not lose yourself, and do not make the exercise about you. Jack, you must shed your ego if this is to work. You fight. You make it about you and fail to see from the correct places. Your working eye blinds you. We will not leave here until you finally see."

Rosalyn's energy grew powerful and big. She was the lightning without thunder as she lighted to the power of the feminine divine.

From the deeps' deep, Rosalyn asked Jack, "What is this place? Where are we? What do you know?"

His bobblehead-storming mind lagged and slugged in a counter punch to the massive waves now hitting the ship.

"Stay focused, child. What do you know?" she asked again, while still holding him upright atop the ship.

"I know…." Jack quick-slapped his field up to sonic and opened his chest to reveal the night sky. His powered-up move attached to the modulation of sound and tonal truths—his portal to the far-off, off-grid, the deepest dark purple place. "I am the altar" came from its tether but not as a sound, and Jack didn't understand what just pierced him.

"Yes, Jack!" Rosalyn pushed, dropping his obsidian crown onto his forehead, further blocking his sight, yet telegraphing greatly his mind's intent. "NOW. GO! Focus. Focus there!" She screamed as Jack faced the heavens to open his chest and greet the day. In the growing chaos of the churning sea, Jack flung open his chest and presence yet further.

At first, he felt he connected to the chaos of the ocean waves. But he caught a whiff of something new and chased it to the truth as the elder ran tethered straps from her bag to tie unique charms to her charge.

"Again! NOW!!!" she yelled over the moaning sea that held a thousand souls, clamoring to meet the teacher's call, making the boat rock, pitch, and squeal.

Jack kept his voice aimed high, unsure, and singing well off-key.

"MORE! GO, JACK, MORE!!! BIGGER!!!!" Rosalyn threw into him and then quickly directed, showing him the base and tenor of the earth-plane physics lesson. Her redirect from water went to sound and then energy.

Jack struggled to keep up with what she was showing him. She adopted its frequency to clarify for Jack where to head. Blind, he tethered to it and gasped. He found its meter through her guidance and immediately met its tone while remaining open.

"Yes," Rosalyn confirmed as he chased after and satellited her charges and tones. She rechecked Jack's current offer, which wasn't quite right. "Child, you are the sonic, and you are the sound. But halfway down doesn't bolt with the required force."

Jack took it in while still holding his focus to the sky with unyielding focus. Again, she needed to alter his try.

"You're here." Rosalyn opened her small ribcage to the heavens, and I need you HERE!!!" She unraveled her all to adopt things atomic that then fired on sub-woofing max—a move so explosive it blew Jack clean off the table. Rosalyn dimmed to collect back her charge.

She ran to grab blind Jack. "Ah fuck," she said under her breath. Rosalyn put herself on the upper deck's floor to see what she had done and undone.

Without sight, Jack was still blind, flailing and fighting all. Rosalyn collected Jack's rumple to still him to skin and return him to the physical, allowing new ways to be known.

As the elder woman dust-collected Jack, louder calls could be heard in the far-off distance, where the ancient ones continued to herald their arrival.

The boat rocked hard against the waves rising from the deep, making Jack's panic grow as everything lost its stability in the no longer silent night. The ship slid and spun in the call from beyond. Whale songs surrounded them as Rosalyn caught a new fire.

"I don't feel safe!" Jack yelled at the nothing in front of him. "Rosalyn! Please. I can't see."

"Silence! We did not come here to be safe." Rosalyn stood to take control, annoyed at the childish tactic of grabbing at nonexistent fears. "Why do you puncture yourself with fear, child? The unknown is not inherently dangerous. Nothing to fear here, and your lack of trust in our Mother disturbs me!" She leveled herself to the correct vibration for the subsequent universal charge as the boat continued to rock and slam, the whale fervor growing in excitement to reunite with their chief.

Jose and Mike scrambled to the upper deck. Fear spread on their faces as well, as Mike brandished a gun. Barely topside, they saw Jack sprawled and undone as his lifeless form waved to and fro with the boat's undulating fervor.

"Rosalyn!" Jose screamed in the chaos while behind him the black silhouette of a monster grew four stories high. Jack somehow 'watched' without sight as his teacher crossed the distance of the boat in two inhuman strides. She grab-wrangled each man with one hand and punched their personalized terrors forged from their fears, into them. She showed them their truth, which laid waste to their unconscious lies—a truth big enough to snuff out their abilities. "We need more time."

Jack heard her say as he held out a vision to 'know' where the men were as they buzzed, slumped, and then slept. His eyes widened, realizing he had seen all this without his sense of sight, a realization that then decimated what he knew of 'truth', as new universal download began. Its ticker-tape sensation clear that ran on repeat within the confines of his simmering black crown.

Rosalyn stood with a stare at the men's bodies and demanded of Jack in the chaos, "What did I just do?!" She was alight as the heavens themselves cracked open. "Jack!" she shouted, her heightened state serious in the shadow of the enormous beast towering behind her, making the boat crash and tumble.

Jack shimmied with uncertainty but immediately flipped to clarity and stillness.

"Oh, thank God," Rosalyn let loose, glad that with so little time, he was finally understanding. She prompted, "What did I do? Jack!" She walked to him and slapped his face. "What did we talk about?" Suddenly, it came to him and he remembered.

"Shooing men," he said.

Rosalyn smiled as the reigning matriarch of the grampus in the water behind her, hit its full height at the ship's edge as a black shadow of intelligence cast its deafening ancient call. It was the loudest thing Jack had ever heard. It was thunder, it was subsonic, and it was as omnipresent as it was deafening.

"Yes, Jack! Tell me quickly. What was it?" The matriarch of all fin-backs then fell, breached, slamming the sea's surface into ripping tidal pulls that rocked the ship and careened all in response. Jack scrambled to right his mind to blank, holding onto his crown, while the vessel became unmoored from its horizontal position. It peaked, then valleyed, and again, again on repeat. The up-and-down motion only added to Jack's swirling confusion.

"It was...," he chirped in fear. Nothing presented to him, so he went in after it as he fought to stay seated upright on the ship's undulating and heaving mass. The entire ship was in pandemonium as chairs and furniture flung themselves from side to side. "It was...," he tried, fighting back tears of uncertainty. "IT WAS!!!" He cried, yelled, and flung his tethers with all his might. The slamming of furniture around him bedeviled his focus, so he tried to level to settings open and found the one he needed. He thanked the universe for its answers as they immediately arrived.

"Shooing men. It is the most powerful weapon on earth."

"YES, CHILD!" Rosalyn said, arriving back at his side.

Jack continued, "The thing that ends earthly fear."

"Yes! Say more..."

"The weapon of choice for the feminine divine is... clarity. The power that burns clean," escaped him.

It was done. The lesson was learned.

"Yes, child." A tear slid down her cheek. "Blessed one, yes."

He had found and pulled the correct lever on his own because, in this lesson, gaining the lever wasn't the win—learning how to learn was. She could have simply shown Jack where the lever was and then instructed him to pull it, but that kind of education wasn't appropriate for budding masters.

Rosalyn doesn't train parrots.

OMNI

As the waters around them settled, Rosalyn brought two chairs to where Jack sprawled in the middle of the open deck.

"Here. See if you can pull yourself up," she offered. Jack was disturbed by so little attention being given to his now very dystonic state. He struggled.

"Oh, stop," Rosalyn chastised. "It's just your body. Nothing that matters for this. Come." She then softened to make sure he knew he was safe. "You'll like this next part."

"Mother Mary in a taxi cab, lady!" Jack wallowed. "There's more?" He started to feel like there wasn't much more he could take. *No. Like, for real,* Jack thought. *I'm going to explode or instantly liquify or some shit.* Jack didn't need to see to feel Rosalyn's stare.

Are you serious? was involuntarily punched into Jack's mind. He laughed despite being caught.

He wrangled himself up with his arms, arranging his offline legs as the two of them sat and watched the show of a dozen humpback matriarchs lift out of the water.

Jack knew dolphins did this, but not such enormous fish. Jack looked into them with his third eye as they passed by and knew of their gargantuan intelligence. However, he wasn't clear how he was 'seeing' it given his blind condition.

As the massive creatures slowly passed by, Jack took them in one by one, towering above them. Rosalyn watched, too, while seated next to Jack, holding the lamplight in the swaying sea.

"Yes, Jack. Open," Rosalyn encouraged softly. "Simply performing the exercise from the chest isn't enough when the universe is growing at such a rapid rate.

Jack tried again and opened himself more to catch its safeguards and the in-beam of their way. He radiated in their glow, learning each song and knowing their truth—the singing giants, the power of sound, and the intelligence from the blue beyond.

"It's their… Is it song, noise, or language? What is the correct way to describe it?"

When Rosalyn bored of his mental wander, she collected his attention in the flailing chaos. "Song. The correct answer is song," she offered as Jack returned to the present.

"Yes!" he exclaimed, catching the right word. "It's their song."

The teacher clarified. "They are a singing society. They have a song for most things they do throughout the day. That's how they know if someone isn't well. If they don't sing, they're injured, sick, and need attention somehow."

A singing society, Jack pondered.

"Hush," Rosalyn said as the next one approached, only this time it stopped and stood still, as did everything else around them. An odd calm arrived.

Jack didn't have visual sight, but he could feel its mammoth presence dwarf him by bounds.

"Mitakuye Oyasın," Rosalyn began. "All my relations."

"Holy fuck-fuckia!" Jack was awed to realize they knew each other. He could feel their familial ties. He knew they knew each other by taking them in and standing in their presence. Jack opened his all to learn what they hummed of so that he could adopt it and become it.

I am the altar, and there isn't anything I haven't been. He said silently to himself as he steadied on, unwavering in his charge, knowing that what was being offered on this day was a life altar—a pivot point.

"All my relations," Rosalyn continued and then rattled her voice to the scrape of snakes and the chortle of crows. Jack had never heard a human make these noises—a spirit rattle, a hyena, a pissed-off-sounding swan! Jack couldn't clock them all as the cacophony continued in scale and volume to the point where he wasn't even sure it was still her. She yipped like the coyote and ran-tethered to posts in off-grid locations that he didn't even know existed.

Rosalyn opened to all, and then they were one. The beasts, the seas, and the skies were all there. He saw them each adopt one another, not as separate but in a oneness that he didn't yet have the framework to understand. The song of the rising seas began its call. Rosalyn opened her wind horse in return.

"Mitakuye Oyasın. Mitakuye Oyasın! ALL my relations!" She sang. "Thank you, elder ones, for your divine spirit of love. We are here today so that Jack may learn more about his assignment. He has asked to have access to information to help mankind walk each other home so that there may be a return to love."

She then redirected to the heavens.

"Hummingbird, come! Our devotion to you, our future generations, come. We ask that you show us what you know. What do you know a thousand years from now? Come. Show us. Show us how to make you now," Rosalyn punctured into the sky where it was received and then answered instantaneously. It was magic—the science we don't yet understand.

She directed at him with eyes wild. "Your totem. It arrives! Jack, you must know of this!" She looked right at him, yet weirdly through him. Her pupils shook as she glimpsed into another time and space. She opened the sky and boomed, "OF SOUND. OF SONIC. OF ATOMS. AND OF WAVES."

The old woman spun around wildly to level into Jack. "Bat, dear one!" she cried as her eyes returned to earth. "You are ov bat, the seer in the dark."

This truth, however, was the tipping point where Jack blacked out, its truth too vast to hold in his conscious mind. This pushed him over the edge, and as the world went dark, his mind's spirit took flight.

RIPPED

Jack awoke the next morning as the sun's gentle light warmed the spring air. He rolled with a groan, checking on what he had to work with this day.

Arms, check. Back, check. Legs, still no. Fuck! He side-stepped the red flag of concern and moved on to other topics.

"Morning, Jack," he said to himself in the reflection of his phone. He sent Thad a quick text.

Morning babe.
How's the bus and truck life? LOL
God, I miss you.

Morning handsome. How'd you
sleep?

I slept fine. Where are you?

I'm in Prince Rupert. Why?

Guess I was seeing how far along
you are until you're home.

How's your time with Rosalyn?
Is she keeping you two out of
trouble?

I guess that depends on how you
define trouble, lol
She is unbelievable

Oh, so she's 'going there' with you,
is she?

Babe. I sang with whales last night

FUCK OFF!!!
OMG, THAT'S AMAZING! HOW???

Jack's phone immediately rang.

Thad jumped right in. "Fuck off. I hate you, and I'm never speaking to you again!" They both burst out laughing. "JACK!!!" Thad screamed. "You sang with a what? A whale? Oh my God, mate. Tell me, tell me...."

Jack tried to keep his laughter to a minimum to avoid disturbing the boat's other occupants. "It was insane. Oh! And, what's with the blinding me!? Is that like a thing for her? Did she ever blind you? I was like, fuck off!"

Thad exclaimed, "I know! It's so crazy!"

Jack quickly interrupted. "Oh, my God. I kept accidentally calling her Voodoo Lady in my mind, and she, like, clocked me every time."

Thad lost his shit in laughter, but the sound distanced itself, like he set the phone down. Several minutes later, he stopped crying hysterically and returned to the call where Jack felt like a kid in church hoping to contain his folly.

"Baby," Thad droned through a laugh. "You are doing the work, mate. She is giving you the business! DAMN."

"Uh, ya. But wow…I mean, wow, Thad. I don't even have words for what I know now just by being with her. She models something very…." He couldn't quite place it. "…Special, I guess."

"Right? But do you think we can all get there? To her place? That maybe…," he searched for the formula, "she's just had a big head start?"

"Maybe." Jack could feel himself wanting to judge and say some couldn't get there, but he side-stepped the thought. "Some might need different lessons. That's all," he replied as he held the image of several paths to the top of the same mountain.

Thad exhaled. "We're super weird."

Jack laughed. "By most people's standards, yes, I would say that's probably true, my friend."

Thad snickered into the phone. "Just a few more nights, babe. Then I'll be home. God, I miss you."

Jack was warmed by his spouse and caught a sad pang in the air. "I miss you, too. Come rescue me from the Voodoo Lady!" Jack pleaded, making Thad laugh.

"Oh, Jack, I'll call you tonight."

"Love you, babe."

"Love you, too."

Jack rolled onto his back and searched again for legs but found no connection. "Fine." He sat up and began his day, once again wheel bound.

Rolling onto the main deck, he was surprised Rosalyn was already busy setting out dishes.

"Oh, lovely. You're up." Rosalyn scooted toward him to help. "Here, love." She chauffeured him briskly to the cabana dining area. "By the table here."

Jack looked at her unamused. "What?" he asked. "We're not sitting ON the table this morning?" Rosalyn caught his meaning and pushed him with gentle teasing, laughing at his joke.

She fixed them a mountain of food and coffee and then settled them for breakfast. The ship cradled on as the Canadian spring air sought warmth. Jack took in the smell of the sea air like he might forget it. He wanted to memorialize it, be ov it.

Sadness reached him over this. *What do I need here, at this moment?* Jack asked himself.

"So Jack," Rosalyn stepped in, reading his long-lost never-ending much-too-sad tale. "How are you doing? Is there anything we need to talk about?" She was the warmth of the rays on Jack's face as he took in her questions.

"What now? I learn about bats or something?" He prompted.

"Child," she said flat and dry. "Fine," she conceded. However, it was pretty obvious she acquiesced in words only. "Yes, your spirit animal is a bat, but you knew that. Why are you making crazy right now with this?"

"I...," Jack eked out.

"Jack!" She had his full attention. "We do not have time for you to... What? Go to some magical mystery school? There's no time. Pay attention. What are you doing?"

He didn't say anything, so she touched his forehead to bring his vision to truth.

"What is this?" she asked while pinching a very specific needling nerve.

"It's a lie," he eventually confessed.

"About what?" she asked directly.

He sighed and finally gave up the act. He deflated and flat-Jacked the truth. "That I didn't know what my spirit animal was."

"Why were you letting people believe it was a crow?" Her eyes brightened with genuine curiosity.

"So…I had a pet crow once, and she was, you know, special to me."

Rosalyn explained, "A pet is not a spirit animal. Don't do that. Don't mock."

"I wasn't mocking," Jack replied defensively.

"When you know something is untrue, yet you continue to allow it voice, that is a lie." She stared at Jack for a moment. "Is it not?"

"Yes, ma'am," Jack agreed.

"Are we done running circles around things we already know?" Rosalyn asked, buttering a new piece of toast.

"That's what I get for side-stepping and being some kind of way," Jack said, laughing as Rosalyn nodded with a mouthful of breakfast. "Bleh. Fine." Jack hated this part—the uncomfortable part. He didn't want to know this part.

"What do you know, Jack?" Several seconds passed. "It's okay," she offered. "Say what is true for you."

Vibrationally, Jack flatlined as he stared vacantly into the distance. "I'm dying, aren't I?"

Rosalyn's smile found joy in her charge's win. He named it as it was, not as it should or could be—the hallmark of a master with absolute clarity ov what is.

She asked, "Is that true for you?"

Jack quickly gut-checked. "Yes," he said quietly.

"And how do you feel about that, Jack?"

He blanked to let in truths. "Meh," Jack finally offered flatly.

Rosalyn laughed, caught off-guard.

"I mean," he continued, "so long as it has a purpose, I guess."

Rosalyn smiled. "You believe you're okay with dying so long as it has purpose. That's wise." She quickly added, "And brave. Why is that true for you?"

In his uncertainty, Jack remained silent. Rosalyn continued, "I just want to open you up to the possibility that this is not an ending but a graduation. What your soul seeks to do cannot be finalized here."

Jack laughed self-consciously. "I'm not sure that helps."

"Jack," Rosalyn now pursued the truth. "I need you to understand that the problem is the portal. It always has been and always will be. It's where the learning is found, and if you review every life lesson you've ever experienced, both in this lifetime and all others, this will be the one constant. So be happy for the breakdowns, for they are breakthroughs. It's as if… if you understood the enormity of this, that this is where the answers are, you would RUN toward problems, not try and avoid them."

Jack was in full, life-movie-run-backward mode, scanning for specks of verification. *What the fuck, Voodoo Lady?* He scrambled in his process to ascertain the truth.

"Jack!" Rosalyn screamed, making him fling a forkful of breakfast into the sea, where below the surface, fishes praised the gods for answering prayers.

"The Lord works in mysterious ways!" the fish exclaimed as they returned God's plan to their elementary schools.

"God!" Jack turned. "Settle down. I was just—"

"You were just about to waste my time," Rosalyn said, setting the line, demonstrating love with boundaries. "We actually should stop talking about it. You'll know its truth tonight."

Jack cratered, unsure he could handle more.

VAULT

"Come, boy." Rosalyn waved at Jack, who couldn't get his chair's wheels past the boat's exit ramp.

"Grrrr," Jack growled, wrestling the wrecked habit named him onto the dock. He was missing out on the best part of himself. To miss an opportunity to model-walk this marina's plank yard to ashes was killing him. *Fine*, he thought, trying to reconfigure a fierce catwalk death stomp into a handicapped roll. It wasn't working, so he dropped it.

They situated themselves into Rosalyn's town car and headed across the city.

"So...." Jack began, wading into the waters of the conversation as the town flew by their windows. "Did I hear you tell the driver we were heading to a church? Because I'm not super comfortable—"

"Hush," she interrupted.

Jack closed his eyes and said silently to Thad in the ethers, *Oh, she's giving me the fucking business, all right.*

"I heard that," Rosalyn said.

Fuck! Jack immediately thought, but then tried to take back or "unthink," which he discovered was painful. *Whoa*, he thought as he began a new puzzle. He tried it again. "What in the...."

Rosalyn slapped his hand. "Stop that. Don't ever do that."

"What?" Jack asked, clearly caught.

"That. That what you're inhabiting right there needs to stop. There's enough of that on this planet already."

Jack thought about it, but couldn't quite iron it out.

"The unthinking. To un-think is to close the mind. This is as destructive as its counter vocal resonance—complaint." She paused without looking at Jack directly. "Is that clear?"

Sheepishly, he queried, "But aren't you complaining now?"

She swatted at him. "It's not that I'm mad. It's that I won't tolerate it. You'd be wise to learn the difference." Again, Jack was being shown love with boundaries.

He gnawed on that gristle for a second. However, it was more the insight he gleaned that Rosalyn heard energy rather than words or utterances. He had known its experience for the briefest of seconds during his encounter with the whales. *Is that how I "understood" them?* he thought. *Holy fuck, Rosalyn receives both the closing of a mind AND complaint as the same. Why? Or should I say how?* The chase was on. Jack turned to stare into the oblivion beyond the auto's pane.

To close the mind is to…. He didn't have an answer. *Yet. Complaint is….* He didn't know that yet, either.

"We're here," the driver said, waking Jack from his steeple chase, leaving him dissatisfied as he returned to the left-brained world. He kenneled his mind's hounds for a latter-day hunt.

What in the name of Betty White in a wheelbarrow? Jack hammered, taking in a church with architecture unlike anything he had ever seen. *Holy Jesus on fire cooking in a fryer…* Jack was awed as the driver fetched him from the cab and carried him to a wheelchair on the parking lot pavement. Rosalyn was already halfway to the entrance as the driver nodded a goodbye and then departed.

Rosalyn approached the side doors of Westminster Abbey and then turned to point at Jack's current failings. "Come on, boy. We do not have all day."

"Arrgh!" Jack uttered as he hustled his chair to the entrance. "Why is this so fucking difficult all the fucking time?" Rosalyn held the door but blocked the entrance as he wheeled over the threshold.

"Just be grateful you're not ov butterfly, child." She touched the side of his head and punched the terror of that metamorphosis into his state, where he experienced the sensation of watching his body liquefy into a casket made of his own spit. Terror filled his every optics and torched his system into a scream while his body liquified into black ooze.

"I am not asking this of you, nor is our Mother, but look how you fight everything, Jack. It's un-evolved." Jack opened his eyes, feeling dumb. "Oh, and one more thing." She again touched his temple and rendered him visually blind.

"God damn it!" Jack complained as Rosalyn grabbed his chair to wheel him into the church.

"Stop it, Jack," Rosalyn commanded with a light slap as someone approached.

"Ah, Doctor, lovely to see you again. I take it this is Jack." Jack reached out his hand in front of him as the speaking voice quickly cupped his inquiring hand. "I'm Father Chance. The order has been anxiously awaiting your arrival. Come."

Jack was pushed rapidly down cold, dark hallways. Were they dark, or was he? But he understood that the answer was both.

"The catacombs are right this way," the Monseigneur directed.

"Thank you, dear," Rosalyn said. "Please, here." Jack felt himself being moved around uncomfortably. "Take the chair. We won't be needing it down here any further."

"The fuck we won't!" Jack blurted, only to regret it instantly. He excused his outburst and moved off the seat and onto the floor. "Pardon."

As Jack heard the footsteps of the monk and his wheels of hope disappear, he collapsed into himself. This never gets any easier. Before they even began, he felt defeated.

"How?" he asked into the dark air. He then realized Rosalyn was gone too. Immediately, he pancaked into a flap of Jack. He was exhausted, alone and left to feel around the stone floor and walls as the ever-present dark grew darker.

RECOILS

Jack sat alone and unhappy on the cold stone floor. His general mood? Cloudy with a 100% chance of fuck my life.

Rosalyn soon reappeared out of the dark, a vision to his unseeing eyes. "Holy shit." Jack blanked with a complete and massive universal download. The spark of knowing something so big made Jack aware that its input will change the entire landscape of his understanding.

It wasn't what Rosalyn was listening to previously, but how. It was how she heard both a closing mind and complaint as the same. She heard them, but not from her ears. She knew what it was ov regardless of the utterance because what she listened to not words but other vibrational information. That's why they all sound the same.

Jack was amazed. That's how he was seeing Rosalyn right now! A new win bounced onto an old tether. That's how we can speak and hear one another without making auditory sound waves. The whole wave spectrum can be available to us, not just the less than 1% that human meat-bags can hear or see. The thought rushed in like a roaring tsunami.

"We're legally blind, Jack," Rosalyn said, standing before him. "But we needn't be. Come."

With his legs offline, Jack felt useless, incapable, and old. "Like, how? Come where?"

"Child," Rosalyn began. "Why do you do that? Why do you immediately move to assume that the universe is somehow lacking?

Why have you chosen that as your default position?" Jack paused to review but then was met with the teacher continuing the lesson. "It's crazy-making. That's what that is. Why would the universe be conspiring for anything other than your success?" Rosalyn asked plainly.

Well, Jack thought, moving to a slightly defensive position. *It's not like I chose....* But then he caught the grift he was in and backed up until no other answers could be found in his mind. His lack of selecting his reactions was the rub now worn bare. He got it and flipped it up for a clearer view and to access higher thinking.

"Because I struggle to trust," he finally answered.

"If you fixed that one thing, you'd fix your malaise. One hundred percent." Jack felt her stare, even in the dark. "So is that anything you're interested in?"

Eventually, Jack responded, "Depends on the day, I guess."

"Jack! Get your ass in the wagon." She clearly did not come to play and this silliness was obviously getting on her already unimpressed old-lady nerves.

A wagon? Jack thought, horrified, picturing a rolling church cart to answer the "bring out your dead" call.

Rosalyn crouched next to him on the floor. "Listen here, love. You're doing it again, and it needs to stop."

"What?" Jack asked.

"You assume that the world is slighting you somehow, instead of offering you an upgrade. Why do you do that? Jack didn't know. "Today, Jack, for the first time, I hope you will finally allow yourself to see. Now I need you to get in the damn wagon so you may be positioned correctly facing the sky."

Sky? They were several stories beneath the earth's surface. But Jack realigned to his newfound way and returned to its healthier home.

"Your chair is an unsuitable position for this next part, and when you don't understand something, you fight it, instead of trusting. Would it kill you to seek more information about something before having your ego decide it's bad, inconvenient, or somehow wrong for you? Your personal 'concern' should be held within you as a direction about what to do next. It's not to be internalized and adopted as a mood. Stop doing that to yourself. It's counterproductive." Her energy then got big. "I need you to know the universe so that you may end your human suffering and move into trust. THAT is the most powerful gift you can give yourself. A calm mind free of being abused by your supposed unknowns and default reactions, personality, and wiring." She hit the next level up, and Jack could feel her booming resonance next to him. It was awesome and terrifying.

Jack scrambled into the wagon, and they were off.

"Holy shit!" Jack yelled, falling into the backside of the unknown jalopy as it lurched forward. Jack tried to focus his vision to understand the new thrust of their journey. *Is she seriously running?* Jack couldn't quite make sense of what felt like a very fast-forward movement.

She nudged in to sit next to him, making him realize, *Oh! Fucking amazing. She's now in the god-damned wagon with me as we hurdle through the dark. I mean, what could go wrong?!* Jack wanted to complain, but eventually, his amazement, found at the intersection of new and wonder which snuffed out the complaint's fire.

"There we go," Rosalyn said, reassuring Jack he was on the right path in the dark.

They rode for what felt like several minutes as the space somehow got darker with each passing second, even though Jack couldn't technically see.

The air was cold and damp. He heard dripping sounds and felt the occasional drop. Drip. Drop. They finally came to a stop. Jack began to panic, which was surprisingly met with silence.

He could feel Rosalyn still seated next to him. *So...,* he thought as his everything else "what the fucked". But he realized was doing it again... He was defaulting to a reaction of complaint and wrong, even though he had no proof.

Silence, Rosalyn put into his mind.

I didn't say anything, Jack sent back, only to realize that he sent his response via the same channel! He communicated with Rosalyn through non-auditory waves.

"Oh wow!" Jack said aloud.

Yes, Jack, that was correct… but please, silence.

With an open mind, he shut his mouth.

In the bowels of Westminster Abbey, a place chosen for subterranean caves and access to middle earth, they waited, training their receivers meant to replace ears and eyes.

Give me your eye, child, Jack received from Rosalyn. He half hit another new complaint in reaction but backed off it extremely slowly, like he had just stepped on a trip wire. He redirected himself back into amazement and took out his glass eye. In doing so, he received the gift of his teacher warming with pride.

Okay then. I see what you did there. Well done, Jack. He was filled with internal pride, and he was leveling up for real. He knew this all along, but now he received real-world confirmation from someone whose yes is a MASSIVE win, not simply a participation ribbon. His win was won by trial and effort, and it meant everything to him to hear her name that as truth.

He handed her his eye, remembering when he had done so with another teacher who directed his life to this very moment.

"Shhhh." Rosalyn put her hand on Jack's shoulder, un-carting herself. The air around him began to swirl with movement.

They're here. Jack noted the wonder in his teacher's non-auditory voice.

As Jack lay on his back, staring into the heavens, they arrived by the millions. First just as flickers above him that began to amass. Flickers gave way to waves and then screaming torrents of hell's fiercest banshees. The thrust of the screaming murmuration flapped and blurred his nonexistent vision.

He eventually allowed their itches of inklings to become knowings that pierced him, that somehow were ov him. All of them. Jack couldn't resist their pull to level up to greet his familial relations where they were.

Laying on his back, he said to the heavens with wide open arms, "Mitakuye Oyasin." The swarm belted him anew. "All my relations!" he screamed into the deafening numbers until finally Jack's vision was restored—not by sight or sound but by their sonic ways.

Jack fell into himself and maxed out his internal radar—the one he used to greet the day, the one he couldn't stop because he didn't want to. There was a knowing in him now and a chase that needed to be won. He screamed louder and louder to meet them where they were.

"Come!" he let them fly at him.

His mind swirled as they did. It was time to know how his winged mammalian relations, and as his spirit knitted into their way, he involuntarily gasped. "They are made ov me!" Jack was a blank of joyous undone, amazed by their flight, sound, vibration, and vision.

The teacher smiled at the new try. "Not exactly, Jack. Think bigger! There's more. From here, child." Rosalyn shuffled to take his skull into her palms. She then rocketed a call of her sonic familial way, the call of whales, through him where he found the call's origins. He began to sing the screech of his newfound familial way, a new echo from an ancient place he didn't even know inhabited him.

Together, the teacher and student wailed and raised all the sleeping apparitions from the catacombs. His call the cry ov bats, hers the ancient wisdom ov whales, the new reverb of the massive underground stadium deafening, formidable, and remarkable in its echos and returns. The subsonic, the harmonic, the inaudible, and the bewails of the primordial eons old, all in a fever pitch that deafened Jack's functioning ear.

He wailed in pain as his functioning eardrum sought to burst, delivering to him the high-pitched ring of anguish. Jack cupped, clapped at his ear, and contracted into a fetal position on the wooden cart.

"Child. Not from here, Jack." Rosalyn cupped his left ear, then bronco-stunned it into silence for a matched set to the dead one. He was now literally deaf, dumb, and blind.

And yet….

Jack's throbbing earache subsided as he relaxed back onto the planks of the cart to meet curiosity anew. He fully opened from a newfound place to adopt his new know, where he could finally hear and see.

With his focus on the screaming mass flying over him, Jack knew each winged cousin and allowed their messages as they passed. He saw them dancing and riding the air, and he took in their tones and newly understood their way.

Yes, Jack, Rosalyn assured through non-auditory communication, thus side-cutting the cave's deafening concert and Jack's newfound deafness. *This is you. GO! Fly.*

It was the first time in Jack's life that he felt functionally whole, and he was awed at his vision's clarity, despite not yet fully understanding how it was possible that he could hear and see in supersonic. However, one doesn't need to fully understand the on-goings of electricity to learn what happens when you throw the switch.

Rosalyn moved her hands from his ears to put one on his vacated eye socket and the other on his forehead—a gentle push in a new direction.

Find your song. From here, she sent. She covered his eye and then removed her hand. Then again, she covered his vacated eye socket and then released it, opening it to the space. She continued this repeatedly until he felt its new know.

"WHAAAA," Jack awed. He felt it. He felt it before he knew it and immediately threw himself down into its ov to review. When she covered his vacated orb, he was blind. But when she freed it, he launched into a world beyond 5D technicolor.

Why?! He didn't have an explanation yet, but that didn't mean he didn't know that he could see through walls, know each color, and feel all forms around him. But it wasn't just the form of things he knew. He also understood everything's density and molecular makeup.

"How the…," Jack started, then backed off from the revelation of his sight, zeroing in on the radio waves from his relations that gave him sight.

Your spirit animal exists to lend you their eyes and understanding, he received.

Jack remained quiet to see how they bounced their song deep into his skull through the vacated socket. He blanked to review.

When Rosalyn covered his empty eye socket, he only heard screeching. When she opened the vacant socket to the sky, to his spirit's guide, the ultrasonic communication from above could bounce into his mind directly because of his perfect journey that gave him this void.

As Rosalyn cupped and uncupped Jack's missing eye, he zeroed in on what he received from that place. Rosalyn was showing him the difference and why the universe had given him the gift of resonating waves that can only inform one with his unique circumstances—a missing eye meant for sight, the gift of hearing from your eye.

Jack finally understood. He wasn't blind. He was bionic.

It's my heightened 25 senses! he realized. *It's hearing from my sight, tasting from my sense of touch, and seeing from my sense of smell.*

Synesthesia, child. Yes. You're here to build a better bridge to those informative highways. Rosalyn had finally placed her charge into his truest way. *Now, do you see?*

Jack broke down crying in the chaos. Its truth was enormous, and its lesson too almighty to his feeble mind.

"I do!" he clap-clamored. "Yes! I do!" he cried as the bats chased above in their swirl.

As the winged ones continued their chase above, he understood the many gifts the world had delivered to his doorstep and how his greatest lessons were once perceived as his shortcomings or universal bad luck.

The torrent of banshees above them ionized the air like a slow-moving hurricane.

Stand and know your holiness, child. It is time. Rosalyn grabbed Jack's legs with incredible force and drew him into a standing position on the cart while securing his legs with her tightly held might. She reinforced his legs, and he stood on their deadness to right himself and stand once again with his master in totem pole fashion. Her body sat on the wagon's deck while she fully wrapped and embraced his stance. He rose and positioned himself with arms open wide, in the swirl of screams. He then opened his chest to meet his fellows, remembering their better, more significant cosmic way.

As Jack flung open his all, he boomed against the screeching echoes and sent his declaration into the universe.

"I am the altar!"

Yes, Jack. THERE! More. GO! Rosalyn screamed into his skull with urgency as the swarm of winged creatures swatted and hit them on repeat.

Jack leveled to a new height until he could no longer hold his charge. "I am a force, and there is NOTHING I have not been!" The massive cave slammed with the eruption of his waves that spanned the full spectrum of truth, naming his understanding to everything conscious.

In this newfound place, Jack mastered a new way, a new inhabitance, and as always, the most challenging part was finding the access point. The access point of his vacated eye, which could hear the world unlike any other on the globe.

He was now seated in his power, that of the supersonic.

Standing before his relations, Jack opened himself to the new world in a manner that he knew would tear him apart. He stood, unwavering in his ask of his future ancestors. *Show us how to make you! Come.*

His teacher smiled at his towering stance in the dark took in the lesson. "Well done child—<u>now</u> you see."

BOING

Jack awoke the next morning in his bed, uncertain how he got there. However, this was not uncommon, given his medical condition, which often rendered him unconscious. He lay on his back, staring at the ceiling, and performed his usual systems check.

"Neck, check. Arms, check. Back…no. Legs…no." Jack avoided thinking further on the matter. That is what he had to work with this day, and so it was. He grabbed his cell phone on the nightstand, still unclear how he wound up back home in bed. He checked the time and sent Thad a text.

You up?

It was 8:02 AM. He had never known his husband to sleep that late. He hadn't yet put his phone down when it buzzed.

Morning handsome. How'd you
sleep?

Not sure exactly

Why's that?
Is everything okay? Do you need
to talk?

Jack's phone immediately rang.

"You okay?" Concern filled Thad's voice. "Jack?"

"Thad. I need you to come home."

"Babe. Talk to me. Don't close off. What's going on?"

Jack reviewed how to say the next part to his husband, knowing a lot of it was better shared in person. With an odd urgency, he replied, "Everything is as it should be. There's nothing to fix. I simply need you here."

The men talked for an hour before Thad had a work commitment.

"I simply can't miss another big speaking gig, Jack. Tell you what. How about seeing if Jonathan can keep you company until I'm back?"

Jack smiled, thinking about the incredibly handsome strapping black man. "Okay."

A few hours later, the doorbell rang, and Jack startled back to the present.

"It must be Jonathan!" Jack yelled down the hall. "Nancy?" Jack yelled again, grabbing at his phone. He sent a quick text to Jonathan directly.

Hey, doll. I'm stuck in bed and don't
know where Nancy took off.
Please come in.

A few moments later, he heard the front door open.

"Hello!?" a husky voice came from down the hall.

"Hi, Jonathan," Jack said, trying to arrange himself in the bed as he could. He used his arms to push himself into a more upright, seated position. "I'm grateful for my arms today," he said under his breath, wondering if his hair was okay.

Jonathan appeared at the bedroom doorway. "Well, hello," he greeted, raising his eyebrows. He was dressed in a smart purple sweater and crisp white shirt, that Jack noticed was hitting him in all the right places—if Jonathan had anything to offer this world it was handsomeness!

"Aaah!" Jack screamed. "Come, hug me." Jonathan made his way to the bedside as Jack apologized for his condition.

"I'm so sorry. My back seems to be out." He added, "Well, and my legs, but that's been ongoing for a week or so.

Jonathan wound his big arms around Jack in a tight embrace.

Pulling away, Jack looked into Jonathan's gorgeous face, thinking, *He is probably THE best-looking man I have ever seen. How did my husband land this hunk?*

Jack smiled, happy to be with someone and not have to lay alone in the house. He internally stumbled on the fact that, in his earlier life, all he wanted was to be left alone. He quickly reviewed the linear distance between those two thoughts and how those two places might connect him to the timeline of his life. Was this progress?

"So, how about we get you up and do something fun?" Jonathan said, bringing Jack back into focus.

They both smiled, and through a series of nods, an agreement was reached. Jack's version, however, was more reserved. He didn't want to be feeble or taken care of.

Jonathan helped Jack shower, dress, and settle back in bed. Then they heard Nancy coming down the hall.

"Everything okay?" she yelled from the hallway.

"Perfectly fine," Jonathan said, reshuffling Jack's body to a potentially more comfortable position.

"Ya, ya." Jack slapped Jonathan, teasing. "I got it. Shoo." They laughed and talked for a bit before they decided to move to the living room as the best option for the balance of the day. Jack could more easily manage in a recliner chair where he didn't have to use muscles for sitting fully upright.

With Jack in the wheelchair, they grabbed some snacks and drinks from the kitchen, and Nancy helped arrange them in front of the TV.

"Let me know if you need anything," she said, returning herself to the kitchen.

"So what's going on, mister?" Jack asked.

"Well, I spoke to your husband, and it sounds like he'll be here the day after tomorrow. So it's just us girls tonight and tomorrow."

Jack clapped and said a quiet, "Yay!"

"You seem, like, overall though, you know…you seem good," Jonathan stuttered, and then swallowed with relief. Jack smiled.

"Ya. I'm pretty good. I mean, I had to give up stuff, but my life is certainly no less boring." They laughed again.

"I bet. But, I mean, more like, you seem to be in good spirits, given…." The balance of that sentence was a circling arm gesture.

"Ya. I'm having a pretty good week actually. Certainly more company than we've ever had." Jack thought about it. "But it's been nice." He gestured with his arms. "You know, seeing you and Rosalyn and having time to catch up."

Jonathan smiled, then seated himself next to Jack, holding his hand. "How is Rosalyn?"

Jack chuckled. "Well, she's… she's amazing. I mean, how well do you know her?"

"She and Thad were working together back when I was assisting her at McGill. Anyhow, there were… probably three years I was around her because of Thad, but I never got to journey with her like I wanted to. I hear she is pretty powerful."

"Says the master journeyman," Jack teased. Jonathan tried to interject, but Jack jumped back in. "Now, stop. Thad and I understand things as you do. There's no need to be modest. Thad says you're a master journeyman, and so it is." He folded his arms with a nod to seal his deal.

Jonathan quietly laughed at the show. "Just like that, then, eh?"

"Yep," Jack agreed. "'Fraid so." They carried on finding a new, just as amusing topic.

"Movie?" Jonathan asked.

"Actually, I was hoping, you know…I was thinking, if maybe… if you're, say, not tired, we could… maybe talk journeying or something?" Jack remained hopeful that he'd get the opportunity of a lifetime.

Jonathan smiled his big gorgeous smile. "Speaking of.…" He ran and grabbed a bag from his suitcase. "I brought you something."

"Oh, yay!" Jack lit up. He opened the gift bag to find a Native Art-looking rattle and a drum.

"Thad said you enjoyed learning about shamanic traditions, and I found these when I was in Saskatchewan last week. Do you like them?"

"I love them." He sad-faced puppy-dogged, making the large man laugh.

"Have you found which you best connect to and when?" Jonathan asked.

"I've never used them. Played them? What's the proper term? Anyhow, show me. Show me," Jack encouraged.

"You want to do this?" Jonathan asked.

"Let's! Do it!" Jack cheered.

"Okay… Let's begin with addressing the space and air." Jonathan stood, a tower of a man in front of Jack, and began to drum. Its metronome pace was steady as the North Star.

"Okay, Jack, now listen closely. What we're about to do…it's a personal journey—an internal one where you have to find your call and your song."

"Ya, ya… Thad showed me some of the basics."

His drumming continued its rhythmic pull and lull as the air in the room ionized anew.

The big man spoke low and soft. "This is where it begins for those who care to journey—an invitation, a call to the universe for them to join you in that space. Our practice is most often commenced by opening the space. Your drumming, rattling, and wind horse, or song, open it." His beats continued to change the air around them.

Sitting mid-slump, Jack found new clarity for what he received now. In Jonathan's words, it was what he witnessed Rosalyn doing. He recalled that her cries and calls, rattling and drumming, granted her access to the off-grid and beyond by way of a vibrational change in the air. It always started there.

"Wind horse?" Jack puzzled.

"Yes. Your personal song and invocation to your guides and spirits," Jonathan said, watching the amazement cross Jack's being.

"Show me. Show me!" Jack encouraged in the swirl of the metronome.

Jonathan smiled at Jack, pleased at the younger man's openness and willingness. "Come," Jonathan led, as Jack sought position, then settled flat to heed the call. Together they allowed access to power and met the vibrational still while the drumming pounded—even, constant, never-ending.

It grew in intensity but not in volume as it consumed their minds and inhabited the men wholly. Jonathan lay next to Jack and opened the space of the room. Jonathan beat the throng of the universal way, where they opened her up more to begin.

"Come," Jonathan again echoed, his resonance filling the house. *What do you need, Jack? What do you need to see?* he continued in non-auditory form. Jack let himself drop into that deeper subsonic cave he now knew, adopting his new know fully.

He vibrationally throbbed, feeling its waves, remembering its resonance and pulse, and now finding mastery over it.

Hope. Jack sent back to Jonathan as he flogged back emotions he hadn't asked for. *I need to see hope.*

Then hope it is, Jonathan replied, setting his intention for their journey toward the place where there is always hope—the future.

TESSERA

Jack hit to blank and began his mind's journey, a shaman's journey. To open to consciousness, to know it, to inhabit it, to be it.

He ram-rattled his grip around Jonathan's drum-beating forearm, and then with their settle, as Jonathan was, Jack was. They gathered and leveled more while Jack opened the sky above them from his soul's way.

With Jonathan lying beside him on the sofa, Jack felt the dark journeyman ask, *Where do we need to go?* He checked for the vibe of the question being asked, but the question continually fumbled in his mind.

Weird, Jack thought, seeking clarity. He repeated the question to himself. *Where do we need to go? Does he mean geographically where? Or in regards to time?* Jack didn't understand how to find the target destination or where to aim.

I don't understand the question. Do I tell you where we're going geographically or regarding time?

Why wouldn't you always give both?

Holy fuck-wagons, Jack amazed. *But, then, how…* Previously, he was trying to understand from all the wrong places.

Jonathan seemed amused at the tumble-down show and quickly stepped in and put up some guardrails. *Jack,* Jonathan sent. *We need to visit one of your future selves.*

No intelligible response could be found, so Jack leveled to a non-verbal agreement. *Excellent.*

Jack attempted to extrapolate some new information that might inform him how exactly this would go as they lay with their eyes closed next to one another. He had some introduction to journeying from Thad, but was still unsure of the process.

Jack. Don't overthink it. There are specific steps you need to take to understand, and you're just not there yet. Jonathan then added, *You'll like her.*

Jack hit the wall of now. *Oh,* he said, refocusing back on the present. *Who?*

Your future self.

Jack had no words. He couldn't grasp the thought that he was going to journey with Jonathan to meet his future self—someone Jonathan already knew!

The drummer added, *And they specifically asked to speak with you.*

Jack struggled with this new truth as he drowned in a side-slide brain flatulence. *They asked to speak to me? Like fucking how?* Feeling massive internal growth being forced upon him Jack hung on the precipice of anger—he wanted to stay smaller than this. This was too big and uncomfortable to know, and Jack had always feared heights.

Someone asked for me? Who? Who asked for me by name? Jack retrieved himself back to an appropriate vibe, desperate to stay in the journeying mind.

The ones you and then Rosalyn asked for. In an attempt to understand this statement from Jonathan, Jack bent his mind to new places as his questioning mind worked overtime to find any understandable figures.

Okay, Jack, he asked himself with his head spinning in dual matrices. *Whatcha got, you crazy motherfucker.* He became physically dizzy as Jack flexed his humanness through the transition toward the future. Most shed it, but it's an option to bring it with you to the future—if you like the drag and pounding of carrying extra dead weight.

The journey took the men through layers of understanding. Jack opened himself, searching his unique way, first by creating a vacuum for new news by pushing out old. *Find me a problem.* Jack seized on it, knowing it could be a quick jump-hoop for bonus points in leveling up.

An odd new thought met his mind. *In this place, you'll be presented with something big and unknown. How would you like to proceed?*

Jack naming for his truest truth said, *I'd like to understand it by inhabiting it.* The universe presented its vibration so that Jack could take it in, consume it, know it, and be ov it. *Excellent,* Jack sent, processing. *I understand it better now. Thank you.*

And that's when Jack saw it. That was the moment when he understood how it was he himself, who had asked to the little stars, *How I wonder what you are?* He took in a new know and understood it was him, through Rosalyn, who asked the future ancestors how to make them and, in the process, how to walk each other home. He recalled the moment when he beseeched to them in the storm, *Show us how to make you!*

In his deep journeying mind he reviewed. *Wait… there's more,* Jack thought, tuning down a rabbit hole of a new understanding. He didn't know how it was there, but it was! Jack spoke it as quickly as it came in. *I understand that the problem is the portal. If this is so, what's the problem?*

The problem is that people are in pain. Pain can be relieved if they understand how to abandon the ego and find a heart-based consciousness free of judgment, complaint, and fear. But here's the catch. In my assessing who needs such treatment, I need such treatment. In my assessment of those who need healing, I am ov ego, which is the very thing I seek to change. It is me who must change, not others.

Jack's defenses wanted to flex, but he continued without allowing the complaint. *I'm allowed to set boundaries.*

The return came. *Yes, but not when they come from the prison found in the concept of safety.*

Jonathan downloaded this new insight by proxy, and once Jack finally settled, he offered, *Your future you is waiting, and she is with someone you've asked to meet.*

Jack focused on stillness because, quite frankly, his mind was blown. His nerves were getting the best of him, and in this place, he needn't choose that.

She? Huh. He wondered what it would feel like to wear that meat suit. He was quite fond of his current one, especially the boy parts. He chuckled.

WooHoo! Colton offered from the backseat of Jack's mind, startling him. He figured Colton had left the building long ago due to his now unemployable skills.

Jonathan stepped in. *Her name is most closely translated to Melody.*

Jack laughed involuntarily at the news. *That feels sort of on-brand,* he agreed with a shimmy. *Melody.* Jack felt its resonance for information. *Melody. Like Mama Melody…*

He lost himself in thought, so again Jonathan brought the train back to the station. *Jack, love. You never answered the question. We can be there immediately if you like. Does that work for you?*

Yep, sure.

Okay. We'll be there once I finish counting down from ten. Ten… nine….

Jack shed the last morsel of his old way, stepped into the countdown space, and opened himself to be with his future self. Within a minute, they arrived.

Hello, she said from a radiance that glowed.

Jack didn't know what to do or think. He unraveled in time and, after a dozen or so seconds, returned the salutation with, *Holy fuck!*

Mid-curse, he awed, noting that even though it was him anew in this place, he was still a man who cursed like a sailor. At least that hadn't changed.

It's because of what those words mean to you, Jack. They are part of your way, and it's beautiful, she sent along with gladness and intelligence. *The people you asked to speak with are here.*

Jack turned around in the nameless space and it took not even a thought in this place to hold back his human emotions and personality. Being next to Melody affected him in a better, more conscious way. She made him feel good about himself, and he wasn't sure how.

It's okay, Jack, Melody sent. *I feel that you're nervous. I can take care of that for you. Please let me know if you prefer to be nervous. However, I should clarify that I do not enjoy being with nervous people. We don't participate in that here.*

Oh. Sure. Ya…Ummm… *Thank you?* He shrugged, making Melody smile showcasing that he was like a puppy to her, cute and in control of absolutely nothing.

Shall we meet with them? Melody offered as Jack searched the unidentifiable room for Jonathan.

I'm right here, Jonathan reassured. *I'm not going anywhere.*

Don't think. Just do, Jack encouraged himself.

Melody laughed at the point of his thoughts, making Jack realize that she, too, could read his mind. *Why not?* Jack laughed to himself. *Oh wow. I'm still funny up here. Yay!* Jack internally applauded. Melody stepped in as Jack completed to himself, *Well, at least funny to me. Ha. See! Funny! Amazing!*

Jack returned to the present, where he stopped cold, realizing his moment of a-has was possibly ill-timed and misplaced. He tensed.

Relax. She laughed. *There is no concept of right and wrong here. There's no right or wrong way for you to be.*

Many words had been said to Jack in his lifetime, but this was ridiculous. *There's no right or wrong?* Jack puzzled. *So, then?* he rambled on only to be halted in place by Melody's clarifying direction.

Right and wrong are always from the place of ego, even when you want to do right or change things for the better. If the ego is involved in any way, it is simply more ov the same, and that's the heartbreak of the matter. Do you understand?

Jack reached for thin strands of understanding, straining his brain. *If I squint a side-brained thought into….*

Melody smiled, amused at the simple weirdness of it all. *Jack, kindly stop. Things here are assessed vibrationally only. No right, no wrong, simply the tonal vibration of what is. It's either loving or it's toxic.*

The newness of this stopped him. *Oh.* Jack took in its clarity. *That makes sense.* His humanness made Melody giggle more, and her smile conveyed that Jack was amazing to her because his thought process was clearly quite insane.

Shall we meet them? Melody pressed and then looked to Jonathan, who rustled with deep care.

The big man stepped in. *I'll take the stray.*

Jack immediately wanted to fight as he missed Jonathan's true meaning. *Stray!* Jack protested, sending the adults in the room into a hearty good laugh.

Jonathan elbow-carted Jack along as they headed for a new place, down a long weird white hall. A universe's long beat later, they arrived at the journeying arc's descendants and forefathers, the keepers of seeds and extinct extracts.

Before them in what seemed to be a holy place, towered a massive presence. Collectively they spoke as one. *We are ov Mapuche, known here collectively as Carvin. I am Ngen. You asked to speak with us.* Jack received their greeting with rapid blinks. Nothing. Absolutely nothing was to be found in his brain. He had no clue why he was there, and he felt deeply unmoored with no known things left. He flustered and churned.

His truth met the room. *I did, kind of, I guess. And I do not know why.*

Ah, the head elder responded. *Interesting.* The collective consciousness ov Mapuche paused to meet the new information. *Let's review.* They tethered to and then channeled to the Akashic Record, which replayed Jack's request as a hologram.

The room watched the past-time continuum as a form of light-imagery arose. It was Jack and Rosalyn! The scene commenced before them and in Jack's mind as a recent recorded memory, now only hours old!

He was on the ship, screaming to the gods, "I am the altar, and there isn't anything I haven't been!"

He thought he would cease to exist from standing in the vastness of this time-looping truth. The scene continued as he relived the experience again, attuned in a new way to the life altar and pivot point presented that day.

"All my relations," Rosalyn sang and then rattled her voice to the scrape of snakes and the chortle of crows. Jack had never heard a human make these noises—a spirit rattle, a hyena, a pissed-off swan. Jack couldn't clock them all as the cacophony continued in scale and volume to the point where he wasn't even sure it was still her. She yipped like the coyote and ran tethered to posts in off-grid locations that he didn't even know existed.

Back in the holy hall of the future, Jack started to panic, spiraling in what felt like a neurological storm. It was simply a swirl of pasts and futures, knowns and unknowns.

Then a wild crack rang out of the holograph as a fence post flew from its imagery and staked itself into the floor right in front of Jack.

The room flashed with urgent care, and the elders reflexed back to staid. They turned to face Jack, who sheepishly smiled. *Sorry?* He was at a total loss as to the rules here. The hologram played on.

On the ship and in their storm, Rosalyn opened to all, and then they were one. The beasts, the seas, the skies, and it was there Jack again saw them adopt one another, not as separate but in a oneness that he didn't yet have the framework to understand. The song of the rising seas began its call—prehistoric and wild.

Rosalyn opened her wind horse in return, singing, "Mitakuye Oyasın. Mitakuye Oyasın!" Rosalyn boomed, "Thank you, elder ones, for your divine spirit of love. We are here today so that Jack may learn more about his assignment. He has asked to access information to help mankind walk each other home. That there may be a return to love," she redirected to the heavens.

"Hummingbird come! Our devotion to you, our future generations, come. We ask that you show us what you know. What do you know a thousand years from now? Come. Show us. Show us how to make you now," Rosalyn punctured into the sky where it was received and then answered immediately.

It was instantaneous. It was magic—the science we don't yet understand.

Rosalyn directed at Jack with eyes wild and hurled, "Jack must know of this!" She then locked eyes with Jack, who stood in the future. She opened the sky and boomed, "Of sound. Of sonic. Of atoms. And of waves."

From where they now stood, Carvin, recognized the tether from the past as Rosalyn looked Jack dead in the eyes and named his truth, as the Rosalyn from the hologram flew into his face in the holy hall, screaming, "Bat, dear one! You are ov bat, the seer in the dark!"

The hologram scaled to dim as peace was restored. The plants in their surroundings popped back to life and again illuminated the space. Jack checked to see the reaction from others, who seemed to be slowing to collect what was just seen in their holographic framework.

The elder ov the collective sent to all but directed at Jonathan, *What do you know of this matter?*

He replied, *I am only the journeyman. I was to chart this course for you.*
But you do not know ov why we're to speak with the stray?
No. I wasn't there.

The senior guide turned to Jack. *Rosalyn has asked us to show you what we know so that you might, in turn, make us.*

They pondered the loop in time this would create when they send back the journeyman with something new—not a new contemplation when all is so flexible in this place. Instead, they questioned, why? Why this new cog in the wheel? Why was this ask etched, and why Jack? The quorum asked the best questions to collect the best vibrational equivalent back as an answer.

Seeing this, Jack realized, in their presence, he could watch things being assessed by their vibrational charge only, with no judgment. There was no good or bad here, only loving versus unloving. These beings had no access to "bad" or "wrong," only a presentation and its level of compassion and love. What mattered here in this place was what the words meant vibrationally, not the words themself.

Words in this place felt different. They were free to hang in the air and be as they were. Their vibration of love was just as important as its sound or utterance.

When a question was sent as a vibration, the answer flew back by the same tube, vibrationally speaking. It reminded him of one of those bank vacuum tubes that shuttle canisters from one location to another.

The tone or vibration of the send affected the reception. Low asks beget low answers, but wow, high vibrational asks return high vibrational manifestations!

Holy shit! Jack caught, understanding immediately that he had been missing that part of manifesting! The answer is always the same as the ask. He quickly twisted into a figure. That's why one cannot "fix" the world when coming from a place ov "the world needs fixing" because that judgment is ov low thoughts.

Jack's brain hurt. *Oh. My. God,* he yammered as an insane person tripping on realizations that he fell through—one after another—while the rest of the room stood there watching the simpleton's ongoing perplexed and ridiculous state.

Jack eventually rewound himself back to the present.

Is everything okay? the senior of Mapuche asked gently.

Immediately embarrassed, Jack righted himself from his mental pull of tethers. He hit a personal vibrational stride of *Meant to do that* and proceeded. *Great. Yes, just adjusting to—*

Lying or being untruthful isn't something we'll respond to.

Jack's face felt the being's words like a fencepost at thirty miles an hour.

Ah. Jack collected himself. *So, why am I here again? Rosalyn seems to think there's something I need to take back. Does that feel right to you?*

They checked how that met them and confirmed, *We shall counsel. Return here.* They sent coordinates to Jonathan for time and location.

The large man understood and stepped in to shuttle home his charge. *Thank you.* He collected Jack and returned them to the earthbound living room.

The silence of the home's space was profound. Jack slowly worked his way back into himself and opened his eyes, noting his body felt heavy and sore. He slowly lifted his head to look at Jonathan, who was also just returning to the room.

"How was that?" the journeyman asked.

Jack broke into laughter, amazed at new universal wonders. "Unbelievable." His spirit lifted to a new Zenith's Peak. "Simply unbelievable."

He fell back, knowing that he would never again fear the miracle of death because what lay beyond her embrace was awesome, beautiful, and good.

FETE

Jack stared at the ceiling for nearly ten minutes in awe of his mind's eye. What he had just seen and experienced couldn't be undone, and his brain was a hive of new knows.

"You okay?" Jonathan nudged, moving next to Jack.

"All is well, my friend. But holy Mother Teresa in a wedding gown, that was…."

Jonathan put his hand on Jack's chest. "Just live with it. Don't dwell on it. It's a lot." Jack breathed and felt his new way.

"It really can be, just like that." Jack's maze of amazement tracked the distant places and loops in time that he couldn't name or explain.

"Like what?" Jonathan asked.

Jack closed his eyes, pondering how that journey shifted him. Was he ov something different now? If so, what was it?

Jack searched for definitions that he fully understood yet hadn't ever vocalized. His voice found deep virgin territory in his brain. "Like, free of bullshit."

Jonathan laughed.

"No, but really," Jack continued. "It's like, as if you just can be… however you are, and it's okay. You can speak what's true for you without others needing your truth to be a certain way." He pushed himself into a better-seated position, noting his back was still offline. "It's like there's a creative intelligence, an almost harmonic way of being with your intuition that's…." He searched for how to define it. "Almost graceful and elegant. It's like their spirit shines through them, and they glow and resonate with this… with this care. Like, when you're standing before them, their concern for your well-being matters for no reason other than you're a person."

Jack began to cry, not knowing why. He continued his revelations, "It's like they see you and…." His cries escalated to sobs. "…I mattered. All I've ever wanted is to fucking matter enough for people to show up for me. I feel invisible and somehow stick out all at the same time."

Jonathan grabbed Jack into a solid, reassuring hug.

"I've never understood why I'm so damaged to this world—a belief they held for me to ensure it came true. Why am I so vile that I'm damned for all eternity?" The last statement flew out of Jack, shocking him. He didn't know that demon still lived there. He had told himself that he was all healed.

Jack returned to the moment and looked at Jonathan to apologize for the outburst.

"I'm—"

"There will be none of that," Jonathan interjected. "You're losing yourself." The fullness of the air around them shifted. "This is why you need to tell your story, Jack. You must get it out to the light to burn this crap to ashes. Besides, in doing so, you WILL find its purpose. There's learning there in your trauma. You will know why its gift was given to you, and I swear if you work with it long enough, it will become so valuable to you that you wouldn't trade it for anything. That's why it's there in you, Jack. It's an invitation to dig."

Jack found a boulder of bullshit to try and hide behind. "I just don't think I have the education… but I did start, and it did flow."

"So listen," Jonathan began. "I think we should call it for today on this stuff. Would you like to get to your room to jot a few things down?"

It was like a brand new idea for Jack, who was still a crumble of jumbles. "Oh, ya."

They shuffled Jack's body into his chair to wheel him down the hall.

"I still got my arms!" Jack waved like they were going down a parade route and not a hall in his home, but it's what he could do this day to stay grateful for what was.

Jack opened his computer and picked up where he left off. He typed a few pages and then stopped to look around.

"Why is this easy?" He quickly reread what he just wrote. *Not bad....so...* He grabbed his hair to force his eyeball toward the ceiling. *I don't get it. Why can I do this flow business when I struggle putting words together for an email?* The universal download he received earlier held that answer, and he involuntarily unearthed it from that last truth-dump.

Jack put his head on the desk, stopping his mind's demand that he question his sanity.

How is it that any of this is real? I know I'm allowing left-brain thoughts—that analyze and use critical thinking, figures, and speech— into my process. The other side, the right side, is the world of imagination, symphonies, and wonder, and while it can't shop or make a grocery list, it has shaped my way of being and has affected the landscape of my under- standing. So tell me? What's real? Am I just making it all up?

"y e s"

He immediately knew, and there it was. He better understood that to flow and create, he had to be without access to any organizing or criticism, not from others or himself.

It's flow, Jack told himself, leveling to its vibration. He tonally adopted his ask and began again.

The scene presented to his mind was highly focused and fast- paced, and he felt like he could fly in this movie-world without rules. He typed madly. The 4D colors, smells, and tastes of this world were so real to his mind.

He watched as his fingers flew, taking dictation from the Universe as fast as he humanly could. He had never been so grateful for anything in many years—his hands working alight with inspiration.

Jack ran his mind through the feelings, betrayals, ick, and mire. He cried streams of tears on the keyboard, letting it all flow out to be free and done. It was an unearthing of a lifetime. It took every morsel of idea and thought to evaluate its purpose and meaning in his life.

Is this serving me? Jack demanded of himself. His personal work was crucial in guiding his principles to assess what would go, and what would remain.

Jack found his truth in his dark and tender-hearted way—ways that he loved because he knew that in the dark is where all creation takes root. He touched on its truth and mystery and followed it as his only guiding North Star.

"Dark is the origin of everything. Everything is inherently good there, ov God there and yet, it is a tone that has been vilified since the creation of God's ideology. Some named as good, other things bad— same applies to the word 'no.' We couldn't function without it, and yet…," Jack paused. "And yet it's been assigned a latent bigoted view that handicaps us."

Why? Jack asked. *Because of the human ego. It's because we instinctively know that our fellow humans like to be told yes more than no, which limits our access to it.*

He thought about it in a newly minted, zesty twist. *That makes sense,* which sent him down a new rabbit hole of thought that he channeled into his keyboard.

Jack received a text from Jonathan in the other room.

Shall we see what's cooking? Smells

good.

Yes! Tonight we LIVE! Wow.
So much to talk to you about!

Sounds great. See you in the kitchen
in ten?

Yes! 

SOJOURN

Jack unpicked himself from the ball of conundrums in which he had twisted himself while doing his best to change the world. He then reached for the wheels of his chair, feeling that old familiar twinge. Jack felt his brain mess with the connection.

Of course, Jack thought, reaching for his phone to text Jonathan.

I'm sorry. Change of plans.

Can you come get me?

My brain is about to call it

quits for the day.

He sent the message that people with Jack's condition are all too familiar with. Each one was an exercise in self-acceptance. However, Jack had begun to grasp that change of venue didn't have to mean the end of the party. Thad taught him that.

Good times can still roll even when Jack wasn't 100%. Hell, he'd had some of the best nights of his life functioning at 50%, and different last-minute changes didn't mean a personal failing or disappointment for others.

Not even twenty seconds later, Jonathan's handsomeness entered the bedroom. "What's up?"

Jack's face, untethering from its usual form, gave all the answer he needed.

Jack could feel his shame and discomfort over being the source of his friend's alarm. *This one could be bad*, he thought, recognizing how hard he had pushed himself over the last week.

He was grateful his husband wasn't here to safeguard him from life's action by setting up fenceposts of personal fears. Jack knew he had to do all of this while he still could. He felt the urgency in his bones that there wasn't much time, and now that he found the trailhead, he simply needed the hours to work himself into its way.

"What can I do?" Jonathan rushed to Jack.

With Jack's face only partially responding, he mumbled, "I should probably eat something. I think I'll have a few minutes."

"I'll go grab something for you," Jonathan said, heading for the door.

"Thanks." Jack relaxed into his newly adopted form, still beaming with newfound truths and places. His right arm curled into a nub. Within a minute, Jonathan returned with food and Nancy by his side.

Jack took a few bites of a ham and Swiss sandwich on a croissant and slugged back a glass of water. Nancy then set pills into Jack's still functioning left hand, which he chased down with more water and wishes.

His left arm then nubbed as well. His neck and some facial muscles remained still above water, but that was it.

Jonathan pulled close to sit with Jack. "What do you need?" he asked with care.

Jack thought about it, resigning himself to his life's way. "Tell me a story," Jack eventually said, feeling small yet content.

"Ah," Jonathan said, perking the room's vibe with warmth. "A story, yes, well….There once was this crazy-ass hound named… Mack. That's right, Mack."

Jack laughed, relaxing into Jonathan's warm body, and began listening to the tale of crazy-ass Mack.

"The dog barked at EVERYONE until one day he met another crazy-ass dog named Chad." Jack laughed again, shaking his head. "And Mack and Chad, well, in typical fashion, smelled each other's butts."

Jack smiled, trying to get his face to work right as it all faded, and then he quietly slipped behind the surface of his mind where he heard Nancy's voice. "He's asleep."

From behind the surface of his mind Jack could feel his eyelids fluttering while he heard Nancy move around the room, shutting everything down for the night. She turned out the lights and left as Jonathan leaned in.

The two men were silent for several moments until Jonathan slipped into a soft chuckle. "You are something else. Rest well. Tomorrow, we go back to see Carvin, and then Thad will be home in the afternoon."

Jack surrendered to the moment, recalling the elders from the future, the ones who made clear Jack's temporariness, which was now very temporary indeed. They didn't have much time. Jack wished Thad could return home sooner.

ADIT

Over breakfast the next morning, Jonathan had weird energy, making Jack realize something was left unsaid. It was time to have 'the talk'.

"Should we journey together today?" Jonathan asked. "How do you feel about that?"

Jack checked for the simplest truth. "Yes. I know we both understand the situation. It would be easier if Thad were here, but he isn't, nor does that align with what they asked for. Is that correct?"

"They seek to speak with you alone," Jonathan confirmed.

Jack wanted Thad with him, but he knew there were no mistakes in Universal Timing, and the timing of this journey had been written. Jack understood this saying, "We should go soon while my body is rested and in better form."

Jack noted their language and conversation felt oddly formal, but then he realized it was the lesson he now inhabited from the future. The lesson being that it's more advantageous to speak using fewer words and to seek to use words that cannot be misinterpreted or abused with latent meanings. However, this method felt odd here on earth, but that's the vibrational residue Jack felt.

They finished their morning routines and agreed to meet after a light early lunch. By 11:15, they both looked forward to the journey and moved back into the living room, where they could hold each other's right forearms while lying down.

For Jack, his access to the Feminine Divine flowed through his dominant right hand—the location of the twinge, the problem, and the portal.

They settled in comfortably and steadied themselves, where they gathered their minds toward a collective focus. The threshold before them was set in time, geographical location, and desired length of the trip, which, as always, was one long universal second.

The drumming commenced and the space flowered, offering new opportunities through thinning veils.

Feeling each other's minds and abilities, Jonathan opened the door for Jack, who then, in his way, opened the space above them to arrive in time.

Jonathan counted down from ten and took them into the room where they had counseled afar. Jack awed at the presence of the collective Carvin.

Holy fuck, Jack splatted before the counsel. He still had no clue what Carvin was. It made no sense how a person or entity could comprise many.

Standing before them, a faceless pillar of white, Jack felt feeble and puny. *Do I bow?* Jack questioned but remembered in this future place, there are no wrong answers, only learning, assessing, and compassion.

Carvin stepped down from their council to stand before Jack as a singular light entity. He was being, but made of something Jack's mind couldn't name. The singular entity spoke directly into Jack's mind, *We understand now.*

Jack stumped on the fact that the wisest of the wise had to take a moment to review and learn. They were equally almighty and open to all new information without prejudice. For them, there was no ego attachment to words, preconceived ideas, notions, or history. For they only dealt with what was.

Jack was overcome by how they functioned from the higher perspective of a narrator—of the observer, not the doer. They understood the wise distance required from the noisy screaming ego, to not be ruled by it and to make new choices from a place of absolute now and the vibration that occurred in the conscious present.

Jack saw that in them, and yet, he was amazed they still asked questions to learn. Jack watched as they heard him from a place of deep compassion.

"What am I to take back?" Jack asked.

Carvin reunited into one and collectively towered over him. *The issue is that the return came from the same vibrational place as the ask. Because of this, your answer may not have been as accurate as you sought. Perhaps it could have been asked more cleanly, more aligned with the actual information you and your counsel sought.*

Jack registered. *They are clocking Rosalyn as a student, a beginner. Wow, wow… holy wow.* The big of that know floored him as he fought to keep his cool.

The council continued. *The correct question is, "Why is Jack seeking in this lifetime, and how can he best achieve this assignment?"*

Okie-doke. Jack noted that the correct question was asked by a why and how, but not a what.

Unsure of what to do next, Jack physically fumbled with the questions running rough-shot through his mind, a move before the deity that they had never seen demonstrated, but it did make them smile at Jack's simple humanness.

Carvin looked at Jack with softness in their eyes. *Allow us to clarify. It's not what you're supposed to bring back, but how. Your you is the problem and the solution. Your you needs to be led and polished.*

The words phased in that manner took Jack a second to unravel their riddle. *It's my me that needs to be led and polished?* He swirled, checking on additional information coming in. *Led and polished?!*

Carvin again silenced the alarming fluttery energetic waste.

Jack. Understand you have been dimmed. You are incongruous for us to be as the creator intended. That is the change you asked for us to address.

Jack's head spun with the unpicking of the news. *For us to be as the creator intended,* Jack reviewed but then questioned, *Us, meaning who exactly?*

Us meaning us all. Everyone.

Jack repeated, *For us to be as the creator intended. That is the change you asked for us to address.* He still felt lost in the riddle. *Really?! Gah.* He shook his head, attempting to clear it. *I asked for this? Ya, but I didn't know that it would be, like, big. You know, like, gah! C'mon!!* Jack complained.

Once again, the council members slowed to watch a spectacle of human form they had never seen before in their time. Jack shook and mumbled, mid-figuring. He had no clarity or connections to places within him, and his searching, he already knew, was haphazard and sloppy.

Nothing was fluid or effortless. He was a circus show of oddities—a plainly insane man choosing voluntarily to fight everything with which he came into contact. He was a man who elected to remain deaf to that which could be easily heard and blind to the obvious.

The members of Carvin held a vigil and waved compassion and understanding into Jack while he sputtered and spat. He began to return to the present, allowing his all to settle.

As he slowed, so did the room. Carvin's energy conveyed that they weren't accustomed to chosen dustups here, and that what they had just witnessed simply was an odd choice.

They calmed the room, and the conversation resumed when Jack vibrationally inhabited himself again.

Carvin continued. *Universal intelligence has written every soul to be a certain way in the vibrational web of perfect design. However, when a light in the web is dimmed or altered somehow, it sends the intention of physics into chaos.*

They paused to see if Jack, whose energy was a Pollock-painted splatter, understood the question at hand.

They asked again. *Jack ov bat…. Do you understand? Can you inhabit the truth that your resonance has to be in tune? If you're mired in grief, ick, and self-loathing, you will never help another because you are electing to add to the collective addiction of "problems"… and there is only one solution.*

Jack gritted his guts, not wanting to be pushed into this next dumpster of discomfort. *I can't,* Jack begged as the whiff of holy fire began to lap at his feet. Jack blanked, begging himself not to be once again torched to ash in the pit on the Isle of Congress. Nothing made sense.

You wrote it into the Akashic Record, Carvin clarified. *That does not change. You asked to be cleared of it. Is this still your ask?*

Jack felt how much heavy lifting the word "it" shouldered. *Cleared of it,* he reviewed. *Am I ready to let it go? Am I ready to not be in fear and constantly pissed off?* Jack wrestled with the notion. It was strong—lifelong strong. Not that he had to put himself in dangerous or unwise positions, but he knew that if he was approached by the "other (political) side," with love in an honest resolution, what would be his way?

Such an ask would demand that question of HIM. And it would have to be clarified and evaluated aloud to himself ov himself. It would force him to face, *Am I part of the problem or am I part of the solution? Fuck.*

Jack knew he wanted to fix the world and its problems, and he had even gone so far as to search out the Divine Feminine's superpower—clarity, the weapon that burns clean. However, was immediately met with the term "spiritual asshole," a thought that made the others in the room smile at the charge's understanding of Clarity. A master's tool. One that is only to be directed toward oneself, not others. Otherwise, the return will be mired in the same ick as the ask. Spiritual power tools used or weaponized against "others" is not ov love. *The change we seek must start within,* he thought.

Jack wanted to keep telling himself that he didn't know what to do, but he did. He flipped up into the seat of the soul to sidestep fear and human noise. He sat in the new truth, now downloading into his way.

He hated the process. He wanted to fight and yell, but the adult in him said no. It was time to stop being right and move toward being happy.

Bring on the love!

Jack cursed the hum within as the old ways haunted him, screaming *Go fuck yourselves!*

The council took in patience and exhaled the divine to help clarify the options and which choices were vibrationally high and contained compassion.

Okay, Jack thought, as nervous as he had ever been. It felt like yet another death while shedding the old skin with no clue what would come next. He still felt the power of Reiki somehow flicking its burning questions at his soles.

With Carvin's insight, they located the tumor in Jack's way, the cancer, the complaint that lay stubbornly still and unborn. They found the lie that he was less than or damaged and that it was the fault of others for his pain.

The elders pulled it from Jack and, in doing so, opened his mind to his nature and who he was. They cleansed and burned to ash all that he had previously been ov. The voice of the universal intelligence filled broken cracks with gold.

The universe then sent, *You are my child, and you are not of those things. You are made ov me.*

Jack felt into its presence, terrifyingly huge and too big to hold in one's mind. It was vast, beautiful, and loving.

With blinding flashing lights, he absorbed as much as his puny mind could hold, while he was rocketed back home. When he opened his eyes, he stared at his living room ceiling while the unwanted electrons from the other side violently shook their way out of him to return to their proper earth place.

Jonathan grabbed for Jack as his physical body seized. Jack's eyes scrambled with terror as he tried to find up and down, right and left.

He simply needed objects to make earthbound sense, a process that took a while for Jack to get right-sided and right-sighted.

The tumble of his way finally found its earthly wear, and Jack eventually inhabited himself again as he slowed to normal breathing.

He noted his change—his vibe, his tone, his everything anew. His mind wanted to hate it. But his everything fell into love's bliss-kissed way, and instead, he smiled. He focused on Jonathan and felt the perfection of his design. It wasn't that he was perfect but rather somehow....

"Holy," Jonathan offered.

"Holy shit, indeed." Jack laughed, noting that even his voice was somehow different now. "Holy shit, indeed."

WAR

Jack lay on the sofa, lost in space. He kept having to find the right size and shape for himself. He felt completely out of sorts, like a living Picasso untethered from norms. He waited until its waves ran their course and left him once again, flat-sided.

Jonathan prompted, "How was that for you?"

"I'm actually…I'm really good." He checked his connections and found himself in the same state as earlier.

"How about otherwise? I mean, other than the physical stuff."

Jack didn't notice any check engine lights on. He scanned again deeper.

"Ya, I mean, fuck." Jack laughed. "Like, how is this real? Like real. Like, how?"

Jonathan chuckled. "Dunno. Ask our relations and elders," he replied, in all seriousness.

Oh, ya. Jack felt oddly annoyed, thinking. *Cause that's just life now, where we can ask folks from other generations for their input.* He laughed to himself and then sparked on a flashing point.

"It's the compassion with conviction part." He stopped his announcement, better understanding it this time. He hated that he now knew where the "problem" lived. He didn't want to know it. Jack didn't want it to be true, but it was. He didn't even have to double-check. He knew it was a truest true.

"What about it?" Jonathan asked.

"It's just so counterintuitive."

Jonathan laughed at the new bulb found its light as he encouraged, "Say more about that."

"Gah!" Jack exclaimed. "I hate that the conviction part is the issue."

Jonathan sat silently while the pump primed.

"But it is. It is." Jack wanted to find another route, but he promised to chase this to its highest heights. He wasn't about to stop now.

C'mon Jack… whatcha got. He throttled into himself feeling how close he was to a trophy. He leveled to plain truth and adopted his ov, the bat, the dark one who sees in dark places.

He put to the blackhole of his mind: *What is conviction ov?"*

He received, *Striving. Doctrine. Judgment.* Jack bounced back to earth-time and consciousness to address Jonathan directly. He felt a little energetic and rattled in his way, now resisting a new gnat under his skin.

"So what? We just lay down and die? Not try to fix things?" He stopped to clarify. "Just NOT have conviction?"

Jonathan looked at him directly, reminding Jack, "You can choose happy and free, or you can choose right. But not both." He continued, "Empathy's glitter bomb is joy and friendship, Jack, not more fixing and fighting. However, that doesn't mean you allow harm and abuse. The problem of 'People doing things incorrectly' is the portal, and you can make them your enemy, as you think they're doing to you with absolutely no evidence… or you can make them your neighbor and fellow citizen. That's how we win."

Fuck them. Jack turned inside out, unwilling to unshackle from certain tethers that defined his everything. It felt wrong to give up and not somehow strive or fight … to at least try to fix it.

He didn't know if he could just give up. *Well, fucking call me Gandhi because I'm just going to sit my fat ass here and see if we win by peace and disengaging. Holy fuck,* Jack thought, catching a new know. *Disengaging—a tug of war, for one.*

His twist set to repeat. *That's how you win.* But the word win didn't resonate with a higher tone, so he flex-checked for latent meaning or ick.

Win… nope. The goal shouldn't be to win but to join in love and high vibrational words.

Jack sat upright, totally done for the day. *Join!?* The word fully disgusted him. *Join,* he scoffed. *Like, I want to hang out with those who think casual bigotry is okay?*

Jonathan snickered watching him. "Join is a powerful tool. Is that what you want? Community? Peace? Because you're putting out dystonic vibrations over that topic."

The phrasing of that sentence irked Jack, but he was more-so similarly engaged with the concept of joining. "Ugh," Jack begged it not to be true even though it was. "Christians." Jack could feel in his spine how much he loathed them. *Bigoted, self-righteous, motherfuckers,* Jack thought involuntarily but then voluntarily matched it with, *Please define righteousness to yourself. Let's start there.*

Jack hated himself in this moment. The corner he painted himself into was unforgivable, calling out his failings and stupidity.

Self-righteous. Convinced of one's righteousness, especially in contrast with the actions and beliefs of others equals narrow-mindedly moralistically.

Jack needed to be done for today, but it wouldn't stop.

" Jack, you never answered my question," Jonathan nudged.

"What?" Jack blanked. Once again, he was in a fit—a fight against himself.

"Join," Jonathan noted. "You were going on about it. Is that something you want?"

Jack hoped playing dumb would fend off the stench of his bullshit. "Join? How? It's super broad."

"Do you want humankind to be one? To know each other as one people? Or do you prefer tribalism and nationalism?"

Jack laughed at the extreme specificity of his question. He wasn't going to dodge this bullet today.

"To be honest, my head says yes, but my heart says, 'Go fuck yourself.'"

Jonathan laughed. "Sounds about right. But do you notice anything about that statement?"

Jack sighed, ready for the conversation to end. "My heart center says yes, we should live as one and we all can be seen as equally correct for our journeys, but it still doesn't feel right."

Jonathan took Jack's hand, "Good. It's because you can't say, 'Go fuck yourself' from your heart center. However, this special place within you is nobody's doormat, and love sometimes needs to learn to say no to place a boundary from love. You're getting lost in the difference because you're still stuck back at duality."

Jack internally flexed with the discord, thinking, *Ugh. He's trying to get me outta the go-fuck yourself headspace while doing go-fuck yourself things.* Jack needed to excuse himself.

"I should probably go write for a while." Jack reached for his chair. Again, he found gratitude in his arms being able to function. For this day, it was a massive blessing.

They settled Jack in his room, where he hit the access point hard and drilled into it with conviction, determination, and then hope— hope that one day he'd change the world. But then again, even that was striving.

If he was ever to find peace, it had to arrive with the idea that peace meant inhabiting the state that everything is as it should be. It required a way of being on earth that can only be found on the backside of trust in the greater plan of the universe and allowing that truth to be smarter than himself.

From his computer, he called "Jonathan!"

"Ya?" Jonathan appeared in the doorway.

"Come in. I'm… confused." He literally and figuratively scratched his head. "I'm super stuck. Do we just give up? Stop striving?" Jack couldn't make the puzzle figure. "How do we… overcome or usher in new?"

It was in its utterance that Jack saw its future play.

"Holy shit!" Jack saw it plainly. "That's it. It's completely changing the game. It's no longer participating. It's disengaging en masse… because they need us, but we don't need them if we decide. We can choose new by choosing differently—choosing not to be the host to their energetic vampiric ways." Jack saw a world born of human values. "Their game crumbles and dies when we stop playing on their chosen vibrational field."

"Yes, Jack," Jonathan agreed. "You can't beat them at their own game. There's just no way, not when they make the rules, operate the news cycle, and hold all the cards. If you think you can best them there, on that playing field, you're a fool. Besides, their way is ov judgment and war. They applaud it. They love it. They honor it—even throw it parades. The concept of sending their children to kill another country's children is acceptable and universally loved. No matter how they dress it up, they love war. The universe asks of you the opposite—the exact opposite—to love without judgment toward anyone. I know it appears to be a defenseless position, but I assure you it is not because it builds communities and neighbors." He paused looking at Jack. "It gets people talking to one another, and it's harder to hate your neighbor, who you see needing help getting their stroller in their car. It's about returning to humanity and getting back in human touch, not a soulless digital one."

"Drag bingo in every church hall each Tuesday night?" Jack joked.

Jonathan chuckled. "Kinda, but it's also setting boundaries and not participating in toxic behaviors. Let me help you a second with something you seem to be stuck on. Do you think loving all is preferable, or is loving that which is loving preferable?"

Jack shook his head. "I was always taught that loving all is best."

"Is providing comfort to hate loving?"

Jack hesitated. "No."

"Now you're saying opposite things. You said providing comfort to bigotry is not how we approach it. Correct?"

"Yes. Bigotry must always be called out and denounced."

"So then 'loving all' isn't a viable solution when creating a better world is the aim. Otherwise, you're providing comfort to bigots and bigotry. At some point, there has to be a 'no.' At some point, we, as loving individuals, have to set the bar and create only conversations with high-vibration words and efforts. It's better to stand silent in the face of low-vibration conversations than to sully yourself with ego and ick."

"But I don't get then how we change things?"

Jonathan rearranged himself in the doorway to look Jack in the eye. "Your mind is too small. You haven't been shown bigger truths, where the duality of the ego no longer exists. You're still operating with a mind that requires duality—two sides—but that is a lie. We are all one. It isn't me versus you, Jack. It's just a collective us. You must abandon duality and step into oneness with what is. Stop fighting the fear that lives nowhere else but within the confines of your mind."

Jack didn't know why he felt sad. "Ya...."

Jonathan continued. "We can't change others, but we can love them. However, loving without boundaries changes nothing. Do you remember your first moments with Melody?"

"Yes."

"What did she say? How did she approach you?"

"She exuded empathy and care." Jack laughed. "It was so weird. She wanted to fix my nervousness! She said they don't participate in that there."

"Bingo."

"Wow," Jack said, amazed.

"She exuded nothing but care and compassion, correct?"

"Yes… while setting a clear boundary that low vibration energy wasn't welcome in the room." Jack was awed as he continued. "She said they don't participate in that there! They don't participate in nervousness! How?!"

"They simply have more mastery over themselves. They function from a different place. Think of it this way. Say we put all emotions and their associated words from most toxic to most loving. Then, all agreed only to use the upper half of the options so that we spoke with care and compassion in our voices. We have so few examples of what a 'no' said from compassion looks like that when we hear it, we're unsure of what to do with it. Melody set a perfect example of this."

Thinking on the matter, Jack spat, "She had my best interest at heart, so that was somehow more powerful."

"Exactly. You want to wage a new war, instead of trying something never seen. Maybe we can be smarter than our supposed 'enemies' by helping them be more loving, relaxed, and open to new perspectives. The world is changing quickly, and we find ourselves in this weird intertidal space, where the old puritanical belief system has yet to die and the new ways have yet to take."

"So, how do we get there?"

"Love with boundaries."

"Just like that, eh?" Jack laughed.

Jonathan stepped forward and nuzzled in for a bear hug. "Yes." He kissed Jack on the forehead. "We Pride Parade our way down every major city street, inviting <u>all</u> to the celebration. Don't create a world where we live in a new war. Let's start there. Celebrate. Celebrate life. Cheer and be of high frequency. Lead with your smile and welcome all who welcome all.

UNITY

Jack's phone pinged on the side table. He grabbed it to find a message from Thad.

Just got to the island.

I was able to catch an earlier ferry.

See you in twenty.

"Yes!" Jack shouted with glee. "It's Thad! He'll be here soon."

Another text landed on his screen.

Please go get naked in our bed. 😈

Jack's soul bounced with excitement. He had missed Thad from his guts. His everything wanted to be with his mate.

He redirected back to the bedroom as Jonathan coughed and stood. "I have a few errands to run. Thad politely suggested I join you both for dinner tonight so…."

"So…," Jack returned, laughing.

"So Daddy Jon can tell when two brothers are about to fuck the timbers down. I will excuse myself and see you both later."

The front door opened twenty minutes later, and his husband's bass tenor yelled down the hall. The sound of that man's voice filled Jack in indescribable ways. Jack was naked and quickly slung himself back into his wheelchair.

In the hall, Thad shuffled his way to Jack. They met and stopped, taking one another in.

"Hi, handsome," Thad said slowly.

"Hello," Jack returned, reaching for his husband's hand. "I missed you."

Their dance of the damaged began as they turned to be together, where they took one another in. Eventually, through a tumble of kisses and care, they found their way to their bed, where they held each other silently without speaking or moving. They gulped restorative breaths back into themselves and joined without sound. Too precious was the moment for anything else. It was the regather from unknowns to face a new north—the one already at their proverbial front door, carelessly stripping away remaining precious moments.

"I got you," Thad said. "You're okay."

Jack then realized how much he had been tabling to feel during a later day, but that day was today—the rainy day well.

Jack cried his guts out for his diminishing abilities and now his complete loss of his legs. He held on to Thad's strength when he thought he would break, and he allowed himself to be human—not strong but of flesh that tears and bones and hearts that break.

The men stayed on their bed for the balance of the afternoon, talking, catching up, and being together with Joy.

As the sun started to set, Nancy knocked on their door.

"Come in," Thad yelled.

She opened the door and stuck her head in. "Thirty minutes to dinner, gents, and if it's okay, I'll head out. Directions are on the fridge."

"Thank you, Nancy!" they both said loudly as she exited.

Jonathan had returned a while ago and knew he was in the house. He shot off a quick text to meet them in the kitchen. They headed down the hall—the festive mood already being born.

"Lucky we got this ADA situation covered!" Jack said, flying into looping circles around the kitchen as Jonathan entered.

"You!" Thad pointed at Jonathan. "The one with the good legs. Go. Fetch us wine!" They all hoorayed, and the festive mood was finally notched up to fabulous.

They set the outdoor dining area as the space found dusk. The food was perfect, and they finally had time to be together, to commune and catch up.

"How did it go while I was gone?" Thad asked. It was apparent to all that he was super curious about what might have occurred in his absence, for Thad knew these two men... and boring wasn't a card in either of their decks.

Jonathan looked to Jack, who looked to Jonathan to begin the story.

"Go!" Jonathan prompted, clearly wanting to hear Jack's version of the story.

Jack looked to the stars and started with a deep belly laugh. "I don't know where to begin!"

Eventually, Jack told of how he and Jonathan met Carvin, a cluster deity of multiple presences, and how these six or seven, yet somehow one, had to counsel because the messages Jack had been sending confused them. He then further clarified that what was wrong was, in fact, him.

"And you hate being wrong!" Thad laughed, making Jack join the guffaw at its stupid bare truth.

"But no. It wasn't like that," Jack corrected, still chuckling. "They weren't making me wrong as much as they said that for the matrix to work properly, we have to be ourselves. Our damage has dimmed our life force, and that's how we lose our way."

In the retelling of it, Jack found something new.

"Holy shit," Jack perked. "That's it. It's in the dimming of our light that we fail... and to change the world, all we need to do is to change its vibrational composition." The new understanding shifted Jack's landscape. "Its vibrational composition is made up of us!"

"This little light of mine," Jonathan sang, breaking Jack's far-off stare.

Thad pitched in to finish, "I'm gonna let it shine."

"But wait." Jack was still back at his stump. "I mean, isn't it just that?"

"What?" Thad asked.

"Like, if we all fixed ourselves and refused to live in their society of fear and judgment, never spoke of it, and ended the old punitive way...." Jack saw it. He knew what was possible. The most demanding ask of himself is for him to be the solution and love endlessly and openly but with boundaries. *Fuck.* He almost didn't think he could do it. He wasn't that good of a person.

"Oh, Jack," Thad said, redirecting his husband from his head and back into the conversation.

Jack smiled. "Oh, Thad." Jack kissed him hard on the mouth to make up for lost time.

Thad returned the kiss with an, "Oh Jack." And then an "Oh, Jonathan," to his ex, kissing the big black man deeply. Thad then sat back and winked at Jack, who snickered, thinking, *you fuck-school, bad boy*. Jack was delighted to be alive.

The bubble of energy in their space perked with something new.

"Oh, Jack." Jonathan reached over and kissed Jack, who was immediately into it.

Thad then kissed Jack deeply and grabbed the back of Jonathan's neck to pull his face into theirs.

Jack could feel his old way of wanting to live big, crazy, and dangerous. He knew the road his husband had traveled to get to him sexually, and he knew that Jonathan had played a significant role in helping him graduate from their own-found fuck school.

There were no pretenses here—only strong, independent, capable men, who knew the difference between love and sex, and they all leveled up for the sexual journey of a lifetime.

SANG SONG

Once the men hit the bed in the primary bedroom, Thad ripped off his own clothes and pulled his naked husband on top of him. Jonathan then climbed on top of Jack and started kissing and fucking him hard.

They hit a vibration that made them glad to be alive on this planet, where everything else was utterly stacked against them, particularly true for Jonathan. Then again, they all recognized the leaps of faith the black community had earned through 350 years of hellfire to deliver the highest, most beautiful minds. Jack and Thad felt their black lover's heart and ways meld as each drank what they needed.

The sweating men entangled themselves in healing and lived, breathed, and loved—the hum of them lifting all higher and higher into a shamanic journeying altered-mind state. Jack had heard journeys with others were possible through a portal such as sex.

Jack loved that he could share this with Thad and Jonathan, but most notably Thad because, at the end of the day, that was part of their secret as a couple. They never had eyes for anyone else, and no one could ever fulfill them as they did each other.

The notion of something or someone in the world being a threat to their relationship was completely absurd. It just wasn't possible when they knew, and cherished the truth of who they were and what they had. They understood their value, and it was from the root of this fact that they could open themselves up so completely to others, and to life.

They reverberated and joined in their journeying minds to travel together.

In a distant place, Jack opened his eyes to find they were elsewhere—a place he knew from a long time ago, back when he was newly disfigured and abandoned.

He heard the pulse and throb from familiar dark dance halls.

He felt the thrill of Major's Mix, and he knew he was young and stupid again… he didn't fucking care. He opened his eyes, and they were there together. Thad, Jack and Jonathan were there… together… back where the drinks and drugs flowed, when he felt young, vital, and strong.

Jack remembered the rush of the club and the thump of the floor. Jack remembered the world and its way back then. He remembered how his friends were getting sick and then dying. All around him….

And the world slowed as he recalled…. an entire city block covered in a quilt that bore the names of his friends and how he fucking hated that his name wasn't amongst them. He didn't know why he couldn't be shown that same mercy in a world where the nice folks stepped over his friends' dead and dying bodies with disgust—and how they were not silent on their way to church. No. They were not silent at all on the subject. They verified what the abandoned already knew about themselves.

"We deserve this," Jack said to himself. "Our dirty, disgusting existence was being served justice. Faith communities were clear, and it stands on record for those who care to know it by looking it up."

Jack remembered the horrors of lives awash in a pandemic where no one even knew how it was spread as young people fled conversion therapy, and faith communities were unrelenting in their damnation and judgment.

Jack remembered more…

He had forgotten how they were but kids and that they were dying, and absolutely no one cared. Jack remembered sitting on the quilt's edge and watching angels and archangels visit a few names. People who cared, despite what they were taught in all good conservative circles and every god damned church across the country. Despite that, some people still showed up and saw our humanity and weren't blind to the Kaposi Sarcoma that covered us in ugly black stains. But it wasn't just cancer that they were deaf and blind to. Somehow they also became blind to our humanity and the suffering of dying young teenagers.

"That's the power of myth," he remembered himself saying as friend after friend was thrown away like shameful garbage.

Jack saw how this history was knowable. Who showed up to help their fellow citizens, who spat on dying queer people, and who vilified those for the crime of living. Jack remembered how, despite all this, gay people were finally coming out by the thousands every day to give each other hope and say, "Yes, me too, and I see you."

It was the rising in numbers, the great resetting of fenceposts as far as the eye could see. And they danced, Jack remembered. They danced all night, practically every night, because those clubs or bars were the ONLY square footage available to them in the entire country where they could openly be themselves. Jack remembered with a smile how they danced and celebrated life because they were refugees during a pandemic. He took in the humanness of it and felt gratitude for the opportunity to experience life in this manner at the intersection of conversion therapy and AIDS.

He sought further, remembering opportunities.

The opportunity to hold a dead baby chick while being called faggot. The opportunity to show up for his family despite them being unable to return the measure in kind. The opportunity to love, party, fuck, and be human; to have the most human journey in the most human way. Jack took it all in, and there it was, right before his ever-clear vision—the forgiveness that he could not previously get.

Jack had unearthed the deep issue, roots and all.

There's no forgiving that. Not only did the Christians vilify us and watch us die, they are still at it today. He tried to think of even two denominations or faiths that didn't STILL have hate for them on their books and in their current traditions. That was the one thing he couldn't forgive and he simply couldn't betray his dead friends by allowing such trends to continue. In his mind, faith communities would NEVER be forgiven, and he held his firmest beliefs in that.

This hate would always be his prison. Always. He was fine with that. It's what he could do to remain in constant vigil over them, to continue to live for them when they couldn't. There was no other option, not in this lifetime, because if Jack somehow couldn't catch the disease, he most certainly would hold vigil and be the altar on which their deaths still meant something.

They mattered, Jack thought. *They mattered to me, and I will not let their memory go down without a fight.*

That was Jack's conviction. However, he was beginning to associate new meanings to the word fight.

When you know better, you do better.

OUTLINE

Agonism: Same Latin origins as agony, meaning a war-like stance against something that isn't war.

As Jack typed those words, he thought about the concept in a slow-rolling manner. *It's the veil or vision,* Jack thought. *Like seeing through the eyes of one's spirit animal,* he recalled. *That's how Shamans get their vision, by seeing through the eyes of another to put additional information into one's mind. Holy shit. It is a part of the taint. It's part of the rot. It's plugging ourselves into the vision of others and failing to see the world as it is. That's how good people are able to be lulled into bad things.*

He juxtaposed all media and all shamanic positions asking, *Is that person who belongs to a group that I detest doing something offensive to me? Or are they just trying to get their kids to school before taking care of an ailing parent while finding community in a place I don't understand—all while being blind to the privilege they hold of not being a target?*

Jack continued jotting notes, sticking a pin in this specific mull while remembering the wise words of Charles M Blow: "One doesn't have to operate with great malice to do great harm. The absence of empathy and understanding are sufficient."

Tacking back to media operations, Jack thought, *It's plugging our brains into opinion-based news or information whose only reason for existing is to make their shareholders money, and nothing makes for better television than fear and drama. It's constantly seeing the world through their eyes, the media's eyes, that put us into that state of agonism. An endless fight against an 'enemy', where we're all the same.*

Jack sighed. He had begun to sense the weight of the drudge he still held for the dead. His friends that he had to say goodbye to much too early in life. A thing that changed him, he wasn't sure if it was for the better. Jack understood that nothing would bring his friends back, and to so narrowly live his life to honor them, no longer made sense. They'd want Jack to live more fully because they couldn't—not less. Being hurt and pained and mad, and fucking justifiably so, was hurting him, and he was ready to be done with that. But damn, there were confusing signs.

A happy Jack—he turned in a smile considering the option. *Sounds fucking horrid.* He laughed and yet became annoyed that he was now fucking enjoying himself.

"Fine." Jack grinned, working his way back into his adventurous digitized tale as the cursor posed cursory questions. *What do I want to say, and from what point of view?* He immediately saw this as an opportunity to explore this 'observer' perspective since the concept kept creeping into more and more of his conversations. *It's not my higher mind where I can go for clarity and to lose the second voice in my head, it's the observer to all that—the consciousness that sees from the third-eye.*

Having found the trailhead and the narrator's voice, Jack continued telling his story. He found details he'd forgotten and was fascinated at the discovery of access points to other parts of his conscious mind that he wasn't even looking for. It was as if, by adopting a resonance of "I'm curious about new news, good news," one starts the reticulated activator of the mind. The part of our subconscious that is always searching and never sleeps.

"Fucking delicious," Jack smirked at its smack, madly typing away at the keyboard.

Jack painted his tales into words and insights. He found access to his left brain that understood complex concepts and could understand tangible objects, like a chair that he needed to describe. More than that, though, he found the right side, which failed at logic and won at elements majestic, vast, and off-grid.

Jack learned he could direct his thinking, and showing up to brand new experiences and brand new people was the antidote to his depression. Jack began showing up for people as he could, and he found purpose in the chase that required nothing more than his imagineering it. That's it. That was the cost of admission—a still mind seated in quiet, that which is not available in a noisy world, even if noisy is presented as a choice. *A monk in the world—a shaman. That is the choice I make as I exit this existence. With the breaths I have yet to breathe that is my choice. That is how I will come to know this gift that I am to myself—in stillness.*

It's not an easy choice to leave the game, sit, and watch birds on land you own, but it's the only choice that isn't ov war—pushing, striving, corporate greed, complaint and more of the same.

Jack understood that we have more choice and control than they'll let you imagine, and at some point, one must choose boldly to exit the game or elect to resign to the status quo.

He felt tired and needed to let his brain rest because its diminishing ways flogged Jack's tether to human things. He tried to relax, but the off switch typically failed when he was the most exhausted. However on this day, Jack was at peace with his situation in life. He sent his thoughts spilling into daydreams of living in the woods, and a life that he and Thad could have. *Who Knows?* He hadn't fully given up on miracles.

His thoughts tore into his tire. *Because if you own the land, that's all you need.* Jack relaxed into daytime-stargazing envisioning how the land gives everything one needs to sustain themselves. The land becomes the primary source, which provides food, water, shelter, plants, crops, trees, firewood...

Then Jack's daydream saw how there's a way of being that comes with living with the land as your constant companion. *It changes you. Sleeping in the woods changes you. It's a return of our personal vibration to that of Gaia, not the city.*

To understand one's greater contribution as part of the collective, one must experience taking their waste, physically putting it into Mother Earth, and then walking away. That changes one's perspective of being responsible at this level—how living on the earth changes you in cycles, grit, and moxie.

But the main vision Jack received is how the intelligent land cares for its inhabitants as a constantly regenerative loving source. *Abundance. That's it! The land always gives. Once you have land, you do not need more. Oh sure, a nice upgrade to the living quarters every now and again, but the land gives to all—with all that you need. That's what the indigenous* people understood. *That's what we need to return to.*

Jack healed his wounded pains in time, but it was a long, slow grind of continually being uncomfortable. It was taking it all out of his head, searching it, and examining it for its purpose and its ov. Was every core belief he held ov compassion and ov joy? Was it ov service, or did it seek to limit the options of others' free will and access to abundance?

When Jack finally reached the political part, it glued to him as a new experience. Jack saw that, in the same manner, he was deliberately accessing the left or right brain. So too was the entire political spectrum—from right-brain progressive ways, magic, and symphonies to left-brain-focused individuals who struggle to change and who will always find their comfort in the sameness of the status quo.

That doesn't mean they, too, aren't without their gifts and place. They are the builders and schedulers, and it is no more their fault for being left-brained than it is for me being right. It was a spectrum where most fall in the middle, but to vilify someone for being on the other side is willful chaos, for they, too, cannot help being who they are. However, this fact does not excuse participation in hate—one can be inert and loving.

Jack saw how this understanding took the heat out of relationships from the other political side. *They're queer in their way, and so long as they do not affiliate with punitive organizations, they have purpose, meaning, and value. If being stuck in the status quo is their way, then that needs to be respected as such. Love with boundaries.* This was an understanding that Jack could live with.

The following week, Jack slipped lower and lower beneath the surface of his physical abilities, and he did so with abandon, knowing the problem was his portal.

On Thursday evening, as Thad arranged them at the dining table, Jack could not feed himself. It was the third time that week.

Jack blurted out, "I just don't want to be an embarrassment to myself. Please Thad… I can't fucking do this."

Thad sat across from him with a compassionate look of understanding. He took Jack's hands and said, "I got you."

"No, really, Thad." Jack was surprised at how clean of emotion he was in the middle of this life-ending conversation, but he knew it was time they talked about it.

"Jack!" Thad slapped at the air, but then he softened to reverse out of reaction mode. "Jack," he repeated more calmly. "I got you." He then pulled his husband's head in closer to kiss his forehead.

"All the way?" Jack asked. "I can't…"

"I promise." Thad closed his eyes. "All the way."

MEDIUM PURPLE

The following morning Jack lost consciousness.

Twenty-four hours after that, he resurfaced.

Thad smiled, seeing his partner return. "Hey, mate. How are you doing?" He gave him a little shake and a kiss.

Jack roused himself, gaining air that was clearing itself from the fog.

"Hi," Jack languished. He moaned, collecting himself. Mostly honest, but why miss an opportunity for a little show?

"How are you doing?" Thad asked again. "We need to get some food and water in you. It's not good to go this long without eating."

Jack was sad they were back to such a serious mood.

Thad went to retrieve some food for Jack, who had access to his arms but not with the dexterity needed to feed himself.

An hour later, Thad visibly relaxed, having cared for his husband appropriately. They lay on the bed next to each other, feeling and knowing that the number of Jack's remaining breaths was few. The slam of that fact stilled them to silence.

Thad rolled onto Jack a moment later and began to heave with sobs, the release of a caregiver torn and broken but still sallying on. Thad wept into Jack's streams, reflecting the meaning of what they were to one another, what he had found and what he had to lose—the enormity of living, tasting, being, and taking in every second as precious and rare.

Jack took in Thad's way. They could not get close enough to breathe and take one another in to share space without separation, to return to the oneness that they had tasted.

They tumbled in gathers while taking themselves in. They kissed, grabbed, held, and shook. On every level, they joined and found the reason the bitter was so sweet, and it was there—right there, Jack found the access point to his holy fire, the galvanizing of his truest origins—his truest ov, should he care to release it. It was in standing in the presence of their sacred holiness with the almighty, not as a servant but as one within the same universe, that he found learning. However, this was more than just a first. This was a door that he didn't want to walk through because, in this one and only case, the law bent a differing arc. It leaned toward an unwillingness to enter or allow, even though that's normally the easiest part when it comes to portals.

Jack didn't know why allowing, in this case, was more challenging than finding the access point. He knew that to free himself of ick and hate's mire, he had to forgive the faith communities for their crimes. He had to accept their privilege and their blindness to his personal suffer-ing, the suffering of an entire generation of gay men—his friends—the missing, and the dead.

The elders of his tribe were no more, and that was a double-edged sword, because while it's super terrifying to travel alone on the road, the upside is that it is made anew from a fountain of possibilities.

Throw the fucking baby out with the bath water. All of it has to die, and that requires a clarifying 'NO,' which always burns clean when deliv-ered from a place of compassion.

Jack took hold of the last complaint he held within him as truth. He looked at it with awe because of its power. This simple complaint, this nothingness of a thing, had the power to destroy, start a war, or pick fights online with people he couldn't even recognize on the street. It was that powerful and that hungry to feed—to log on, yell, and be right in its position-fed stance. *The mind ruled by ego will be 'right' at all costs. Being right at all costs is why we have war. Peacemakers bring Peace. Warriors bring war. Which am I?*

But then Jack compared his truest self with that inside him. Which version of Jack could he be proud of? Which one, in the end, would matter?

He put the plain answer to his mind and watched his need for a different outcome dance on the palm of his hand—a complaint, a wisp dancing on his hand, turning from plum to peach and then to ash white. Watching the thing evaporate into the nothingness it was, Jack's happy, his carefree and his joy returned.

Thad was there with him in this outer space daydream. He felt and saw him, and before them, they saw themselves as kids laughing together on the beach.

It was a beautiful daydream…

Jack saw them in his mind as they ran down the shoreline chasing, screaming, and laughing. Freedom was found in the sunbeams of light telling them they were okay.

Not yet crimes against humanity—not yet.

GRADUATION DAY

The following midnight, everything was normal.

Thad arranged for Joy to be taken by a trustworthy friend, and he left Nancy a note and an executed deed to the home on the kitchen counter. He then dressed, showered, and did the same for Jack, who languished, a bobble of semi-conscious mush. They both looked handsome, clean, and fresh like the day they joined in holy matrimony.

Thad took out two lapel pins with a design of a lit candle in a circle, and as he attached them to their lapels he explained the meaning to Jack.

"Finally had these made. Guess just in time."

Jack could feel and hear his partner, but his eyes typically failed to open, which greatly helped in shielding him from the continuous onslaught of painful stimuli.

"I am on my journey for one." Jack heard. "I am working toward ending trauma and embodying the understanding that everyone on the planet rings of one vibration. I am the change and it all begins with me. I am, and now with you… well, the Anam Cara will take care of that."

Jack felt himself being kissed lightly even though he couldn't return the gesture. It was clear why they were dressing.

"This little light of ours," Thad sang as he finished pinning them to their suits. "My love. May this planet know peace again before man made himself into an unconscious god. May we do better. May we shine this light, share this light saying, no more. I will war, no more. I will hate, no more. I will bring nothing into existence other than high vibration words. It's possible Jack. I know it is."

Jack then felt them moving. He knew he was in his wheelchair, but didn't know exactly where Thad was taking them until he heard the elevator doors slide open.

"This little light of mine… I'm gonna let it shine." Thad's baritone voice echoed in the small enclosed space. When the doors slid closed and the elevator car began to go up, Jack knew why they were headed there. He smiled in the elevator up to the attic, where Thad and a death doula had prepared the space for this eventuality.

Thad helped Jack onto the mattress on the floor and laughed mid-stumble. Jack could feel his eyes flutter as his husband said, "I thought you were supposed to be the strong one!"

Jack felt Thad properly arrange him and then climb on top of his hips.

Thad kissed Jack deeply. "You never read the last chapter of Zenith's Peak, so here goes." He cracked open a copy of his book and began to read while Jack found the slip that allowed him to observe their final few moments together from a higher place.

"Chapter forty-seven," Thad began.

Telos: The final cause of an organ, entity, or work of human art.

In the end, we will not regret what we did but rather what we didn't do. The life we didn't live is ultimately the tragedy we all will face—and here, in my life's embodiment of work, I will make my final case for a life lived summiting our own personal Zenith's Peak, our personal mountain to climb.

My upbringing was difficult, made even more so by the unexpected death of my mother, my only caregiver. As I made my way through the foster care system, I'd often find myself in an unexplainable situation that ranged from abusive to empowering, all while gnawing on this need for things named Thad to be different.

I told myself untrue things while seeking out the unbelievable that fed my curious mind. It was as if knowing some led to wanting to know more, almost like an addiction. I learned to trust things differently, and not just the physical—something I had been given access to at a very early age, and if it's a thing a child can learn, my hope is that we'll all be open to its call.

One of my graduating thesis papers at McGill focused on our energetic access across trans-generational boundaries. It was co-authored by McGill University's professor of Anthropology, Doctor Rosalyn Thames, my guide and guru. She is a woman who has shown me things I cannot explain, yet they are there.

I could tell you of the worlds I have visited and the experiences I have had contained in little more than what appears to be an afternoon nap, but what I'm speaking of is a slightly different channel: a portal to discovery.

Throughout my young adult life, I crashed and burned, succeeded, and faltered more than I can name. Through much of it, my friends and partners tried to show me balance. However, something was always slightly off, and it took my relationship with Jonathan ending for me to see that my internal need to own and possess others was feeding me from all the wrong places, but was it something I wanted to give up? Was my need to possess another and hold the balance of their life in my hands a character defect? A failure on my part—a failure of my creation or of my Creator?

Probably yes to most. However, what if I could find someone whose assignment this lifetime was to be possessed? To be owned. To be beaten mercilessly. Who's his match?

That's the thing about a life lived reaching for Zenith's Peak. We get to make new ways to be in the world and consciously decide who we want to be and what life we want to make, with no rules other than the Golden One.

Ultimately, I decided not to abandon my thirst for a unity such as that because somewhere in me, I knew that in this lifetime, I would find it; I would find him. I would find the one who was so wholly ov love that he *came to speak its name to power, because I've read all your high-fucking-minded books—and as long as faith communities operate with hate, one must be anti-Christ to be ov love. That's who I seek. That's what I seek. To set free those oppressed by faith-sanctioned bigotry found in Leviticus 20:13, a thing that calls for our executions and a thing that has been used as a cudgel against us for far too long!*

This grasp. This need. It's a huge part of how I operate, as it is the only salve for my long ago abandoned mind. For me, it is security. To tether as one with another like that in a holy way, even for a moment, would be the fulfillment of my life's work. However, I do not doubt that such a thing would be fleeting, for if a person were to take such a position and stand boldly against every God-damned Mormon, Christian, and practicing Jew who places their hands on a book of oppressions, curses and known evil, there is no doubt in my mind that they wouldn't be long for this earth. Those who hold privilege do not self-regulate prejudice out of existence. No. Not when it serves them. They fight for it, and protect it; otherwise, in this day and age, we would see the tiniest allotment of recognizing our humanity. But they don't. Even to the black community and all the practicing Jews, the humanity of those born onto the queer spectrum isn't seen in their books of worship; that's how invisible our humanness is. Even the marginalized marginalize us, and it is time to name it all as their shame.

Many were freed from Auschwitz during the Second World War, but not us. The queer did not get to be free as the Jews because we were still a crime. Still are. A thing that could be simply fixed if even one of the twenty-five versions of the Bible being sold on the corner said we were human, decent, or good rather than "an abomination" in the eyes of God. That is our ask. A version of your holy book that names us as human. It's a start; otherwise, if you cannot meet us there, we will have to seek to have the Bible removed from all public spaces.

We don't want this war—we simply want to exist, but so long as the "correct and blessed" use hate, they cannot be seen as good, ever. Let's start there. Remember: The only ones to fear are the ones with a mouthful of fear, something the evolved ones never speak or utter into existence. High-vibration individuals never employ fear, speak of hate, or give its dark vibration air. We are better than that, and high-minded thoughts must begin to find their way into high-vibration conversations. Conversations that encourage, bless, and see the humanity in others. Always.

All my life, I have searched for my Zenith's Peak, and I understand that to remain true to myself and to my commitment to live as I am designed, I have to see if it is possible. I don't know that it is, but when I find it, I will be able to die the happiest man on earth. Even if I only have five minutes of it.

I would kill for that.

I would die for that.

Jack heard Thad cry and wipe the tears from his face saying, "Five minutes". There was other movement which Jack took in as clicks on a smartphone.

Silent motionless moments went by as the room found a reverent tone. Jack knew what this was, and in the perfect silence he reviewed it all. The beautiful awful—life.

When the alarm struck its bell, Jack felt Thad slowly silence it, then lean down and kiss him. Thad placed their left ears together, put the barrel of a pistol to his temple, and with a single shot, ended both their lives.

HOME

In a flash that sang of hallelujah, Jack was free. He beamed of joy and turned to feel Thad.

"Babe!" Jack yelled, hugging him quickly while their molecules still recognized a glinting thread of form.

Thad smiled and said, "We're super weird."

Jack clapped and beamed joy into his love. "And thank God for that… for that has made all the difference."

"You want to give this one another go?" Thad pointed at the earth, beginning to fade in the distance.

They kissed, and as they went to their proper places, Jack lovingly laughed and said, "Fuck no. I don't want to be a pioneer to density anymore." Jack paused a moment, remembering, and added, "Besides, I've seen the future, and it is beautiful."

They set their intention to be ov their next journey, calling out geographical destination, time, and how soon to arrive.

They had done their work and learned dense things, part of which meant loving themselves enough to say no. No, I will not be ov that density that shames or harms in judgment while calling itself righteous. I will only be ov high vibration and love, and I will not be co-opted into the wars of others. So, no. As a mother says to a child from a place of absolute adoration, "No. Enough. It ends with me on my journey for one, assessing only from non-judgment and responding with compassion for their pain.

There is a place behind the guardrail that cheers and welcomes others to the same shore—the shore carefree of latent bigotry and hate that sees the suffering of others and recognizes that prejudice cannot stand. Ever."

"Love with loving boundaries," Jack recalled. *That's where we're headed, so be ov joy and celebrate all, for we only evolve in one direction.*

From Jack and Thad's new vantage point, they saw how everything on earth was either love or a cry for love. Nothing else. That's all there was—hurt people hurting people in need of healing from new thoughts that modeled something novel. The solution is simple but not always easy.

They grabbed their final atoms together and allowed death's grace to take them. They thanked each other for the journey as they held hands and walked the other home knowing that they had done their work.

"See you soon, handsome." Thad winked. "I will always love you."

"See you soon. And Thad?" Jack asked.

"Ya?"

"Thank you for making Earth seem less foreign to me."

A NOTE FROM THE AUTHOR

If you have enjoyed the *Journey of a Dark Shaman Trilogy*, watch for the publication of the next book in the series, *Journey of a Light Shaman, Book 1, Zenith's Peak*. The adventure continues but is told from a higher and more sinister place, the devilishly weird world of Thaddeus Harold Pierson-Daw.

If you enjoyed reading *Made Ov Me*, please leave a review on Amazon. I read every review, and they help new readers discover my books.

Foreign To Me and *Broken Like Me,* books I and II in *The Journey of a Dark Shaman* trilogy, are available on Amazon in Kindle and print formats. The audiobook versions are also available for purchase through both Amazon and Audible. To see all of the books in this series and my fictional series *The Language in Light*, visit my author page at amazon.com/author/dale-allen-rowse

I also invite you to check out my YouTube channel, where I cover many of the topics discussed in *Journey of a Dark Shaman Trilogy* and fictional *The Language in Light* book series, as well as topics ranging from shamanism to manifesting and evolving in this ever-expanding reality in which we exist. Visit and subscribe at YouTube.com/DaleAllenRowse

For more information, visit: www.DaleAllenRowse.com

ABOUT THE AUTHOR

Dale Allen-Rowse always knew he was a creator and a storyteller. However, it wasn't until Celine Dion hired him as an original cast member for her show 'A New Day' that he understood his calling. During the almost year-long creation of Celine's Las Vegas show, Dale's vision for storytelling, narrative, and fantasy emerged. He worked for three years under the direction of Dion's director, Franco Dragone, the creative genius behind many of the Cirque de Soleil shows. From that relationship, Dale discovered his voice.

In 2005, Dale left Celine's employment, ending an eighteen-year professional theatre performing career to pursue a new life in real estate. Within three years of becoming a real estate agent, Dale was awarded top honors for individual sales volume for RE/MAX and opened a brokerage firm.

After a twenty-year career as an agent and real estate coach, Dale is adding new passions to his interests, including his spiritual life as a shamanic practitioner and student of core shamanism.

Dale channels his books using 'Automatic Writing,' which he discusses on YouTube.com/DaleAllenRowse channel – as well as many of the topics covered in his books, such as personal evolution, spiritual energy work, core shamanism, manifesting, and evolving. Plus, his talks are set to a disco beat, and that's not nothing.

Dale and his husband John live on a five-acre ranch in Mountain Center, California. They currently have five dogs with a miniature donkey possibly in their future. Other things that keep Dale occupied are his quilts – you can see his work online as the Quilting Cowboy – and his day job as a real estate sales educator and coach.